Checkpoint USSR

The truck with the sacks of potatoes was behind a line of vehicles that stopped and advanced as each one went through the checkpoint. Huddled in concealment in the back of the truck, Nile Barrabas tightened his hold on the H&K machine pistol when he could tell that his vehicle had just rolled up and was next in line. He heard the soldiers asking sharp questions, and then the resounding thuds as the top sacks were dragged down and thrown on the ground.

The massive pile grew smaller as the soldiers resolutely heaved the bags off. An exasperated tug sent an entire stack toppling and exposed Barrabas. The soldier had taken a step back to avoid the tumbling sacks, and when he next looked up, he was staring right into Barrabas's cold gaze. But he had no time to act on his surprise. The H&K coughed hoarsely.

SOLDIERS OF BARRABAS

THE BARRABAS RAID

JACK HILD

A GOLD EAGLE BOOK FROM
WORLDWIDE.

TORONTO • NEW YORK • LONDON • PARIS
AMSTERDAM • STOCKHOLM • HAMBURG
ATHENS • MILAN • TOKYO • SYDNEY

First edition July 1988

ISBN 0-373-61625-2

Special thanks and acknowledgment to
John Preston for his contribution to this work.

1

Something about the scene reminded Nile Barrabas of Vietnam. He was standing on a corner on the East Side of New York, watching a ragged line of demonstrators marching quietly on the other side of the street. Carrying homemade signs, they kept as close to the United Nations building as was allowed. A bored detachment of New York City police looked on. They could afford to be bored this time. Most of the protesters seemed elderly, many of them at least sixty. There wasn't going to be any violence from them: they were there as witnesses to injustice, even if the world wanted to ignore what they had to say.

Their cause meant nothing to the hustling crowds of New Yorkers on their way to and from the soaring office towers of Manhattan. And suddenly Nile realized what had evoked the flashing scenes of battle. In Nam he had seen courage and, when even energy was gone, a sheer determination to not give up. Without waving placards, or shouting and shoving, the demonstrators were showing a willingness to go against the tide of indifference. Nile knew that year by year they would remind the world of their country's plight, and that it meant a quiet resolve to state their case even if it seemingly accomplished nothing. It was a battle, too, against the daily personal worries that can slowly erode a larger cause.

Most of the placards bore one message: August 23—A Day of Infamy. Free Latvia!

That was the anniversary of the date when the fate of the tiny Baltic states—Latvia, Estonia and Lithuania—was determined, a fate that meant subservience to the USSR.

At the end of the Second World War, the victors turned to matters of greater importance to them than the fate of three countries that had been swallowed up by the Soviet empire.

While Baltic émigrés had tried to keep alive the demand to have their countries freed, the United States and Great Britain had only paid lip service to the Baltic states, allowing them to maintain separate embassies in Washington and London as mere symbols of the freedom that had once been.

The people marching and persevering in the August heat of Manhattan knew they weren't going to be heard by the bureaucrats in the skyscraper. They knew they were not good copy for the newspapers that were all fighting on one or the other side of the Nicaraguan war. Armies of television technicians wouldn't intrude with their cameras to record a straggling line of people proclaiming their dignity.

Nile stared, thinking that some of the passersby eyed the protesters as though they were the types of lunatics who make life a hassle for the everyday New Yorker. Most likely they didn't even know where Estonia, Latvia and Lithuania were.

The three Baltic states line the east coast of the Baltic Sea, south of Finland, east of Sweden, north of

Poland. Their geography had been unlucky for them throughout their history because of their closeness to the Russian empire and its expansionist policies, which had only continued after the Bolshevik revolution.

Nile mentally saluted the men and women who kept alive the memory of the independence of their birthplaces and began to walk away. Moving through the throngs of New Yorkers, he reflected that he was thankful he was an American, born and raised and living in the most powerful country in the world. His freedom was protected by the power and wealth of the United States, and especially by its democratic institutions.

Barrabas wouldn't hesitate to forcibly protect any erosion of the liberty of America: he was a man who fought for democracy every day of his life. He could only hope that the indifferent crowd would defend its liberty, too, if it were directly challenged.

A man like himself, trained in war, was prepared to fight. In a profound sense it meant acting according to his nature. But what is it that takes a regular person out of society and turns him or her into a patriot? Nile wondered, scanning the faces of the people on the New York sidewalk. He couldn't figure it out. He never had, and was astonished that it happened.

CERTAIN QUARTERS OF RIGA, the capital of Latvia, survived the terrible bombings of the Second World War. The prewar style of the cosmopolitan capital is still evident in the architecture of the city, which was once a center of trade and commerce and art.

Easily the most colorful city in the modern Soviet Union, Riga sits at the head of the Gulf of Riga, a large inlet off the Baltic Sea, only a couple of hundred kilometers from Finland—and the West.

That closeness is evident in the style everywhere. The women seen in the heart of the city dress with more grace and accented beauty than anywhere else in the Soviet empire. There is no evidence of the drab grayness of Moscow's women, nor of the shabby poverty of Kiev. Riga is a city on the edge of Europe, and it shows a lot in the feminine apparel, in the lines of the skirts and the cut of the blouses.

At the sidewalk cafés, bright with colorful umbrellas, groups of people gather to drink thick Turkish-style coffee and wine and talk with animation.

Many of the cafés in the old quarter line a small square. According to local legend, the Teutonic Knights, who ruled Latvia in medieval times, would gather there to pass on to their initiates the privileges and responsibilities of manhood.

A conquered people often try to survive by ignoring their realities. They turn away from the soldiers who march by and forget the foreign names imposed on their streets. Despite the official name of the square, the people at the tables knew it as Knighthood Square. University students would still go there as part of their forbidden pranks and playfully induct one another into the ranks of the Teutonic Knights of old as a part of their springtime rituals.

The Russians hated that. They didn't like the fact that the citizens of Riga still remembered and revered their past role as one of the great trading cities of ancient times and that they romanticized their part in world history so much. During Stalin's time the Knighthood Square ceremonies had been forbidden, and the few students who had dared to appear to maintain the traditions had found themselves sent off to the worst of the labor camps—and even death—for remembering anything that had to do with any time when the Latvians had been anything but subjects of the Russian Empire.

It was the university's vacation period, and the only students in sight were those enjoying the August heat in the pleasant shade of the cafés with other young people. Not that they would be sent off to labor camps anymore for their pranks. *Glasnost*, the policy of "openness," was the style set in Moscow. The Soviet Union was trying to show the West that it was no longer as rigid as it had been. Especially not the way it had been in the old Stalin days. How could the authorities complain about the stylish cut of the Latvian women's clothing when their own leader's wife wore Paris fashions?

Life was better, it was easier, and there was less to worry about. The jovial throng in Knighthood Square was happy to forget that it had been otherwise.

Suddenly, off to the side of the square, there appeared a line of five people who marched with a particularly sober determination that made them noticeable among the crowd of strollers.

"What are they doing here, do you think, Janis?" a young woman asked her companion when she saw the half-dozen elderly people come into view.

Janis Valters, the young man whom she'd asked, looked over to where she was pointing and feigned indifference. That was his own style, one that matched the casual and careless appearance of his clothes and his less-than-conventional hairstyle.

"Just a bunch of people looking for something to do, Koren," he said, dismissing the sight.

He went back to sipping his thick coffee.

"Oh, no!" Koren said suddenly. Janis looked at her, wondering what was bothering her now. He followed Koren's gaze and saw that the people, all of whom seemed well past middle age, had unfurled a long banner. The banner simply showed a date: August 23, 1939.

Quiet descended on the noisy crowds at the cafés. A shocked silence that was followed by an almost sullen resentment of the sudden and unwanted intrusion of reality into their lives.

Just what the reality was came home to Janis when he saw the uniformed militia move into action. *Glasnost*—the new openness that was touted constantly in the media—had its limits, apparently. Certain reminders were not going to be tolerated.

It looked as though the public retribution would be sugarcoated, however. There were only three of the militiamen. A few years ago there would have been dozens of them to stamp out the slightest hint of an uprising, Janis reflected. But *glasnost* wouldn't encourage that kind of show of force, which might be caught by a Western video camera. The image of totalitarianism wasn't one the new regime in Moscow wanted to have on democratic television.

Janis saw that Julijis Stucka was the leader of the quiet attack, and he sneered when he recognized him. At one time Janis had worshiped Julijis, who was only three years older than he. But that had been enough difference in their ages for Janis to turn the older boy into a full-fledged hero.

When they'd been in school, Janis had imitated Julijis's choice of clothing. Janis played soccer for hours on end after watching Julijis star on the Latvian junior championship team. When Julijis decided to enter the University of Riga, Janis vowed he'd follow.

Without an older brother of his own, Janis fastened on Julijis as his role model. Every nod the other boy gave him was a treasured moment for a week afterward. When Julijis deigned to share a conversation with Janis, the younger boy sweated with worry that he'd sound stupid.

When had it all changed? What had really happened? Janis tried to remember back to those days in gymnasium—the local equivalent of high school—and he remembered when he and the others first started to share magazines and newspapers from the West. In Latvia they were very close to the television and radio broadcasts of Finland, Sweden and even West Germany. They could get more information from the West than most other people in the Soviet Union.

In addition, Riga was a major international seaport, and there were always ways for fishermen to sneak in publications.

Julijis had been a leader in the Young Pioneers, the Communist youth organization, and Janis had automatically joined. There the youngsters had been taught all about the terrible drawbacks of capitalism, balanced by unrestrained propaganda in praise of Communism.

But in the Western publications that Janis and his friends were reading for their music gossip and for hints to what was the up-and-coming group of the day, there were strange stories about Russian involvement in conspiracies against many free people. Then, eventually, the magazines carried news that Soviet troops had invaded Afghanistan, and it was presented in a different light than in the papers at home.

That knowledge changed all kinds of things in Janis's life. It set off small tremors in his mind as the pieces of a huge jigsaw puzzle began to fall into place.

He began to wonder about his uncle Mikelis, who no one wanted to talk about. He had evidently been a fine and noble man, one of the many who had fought in the Second World War, when Latvia had been a battlefield overrun by the Germans. But there had always been a hint of something different in the way that people talked about Uncle Mikelis.

There was an embarrassment Janis could sense in those relatives and family friends who were in favor of the Russian occupation, but those who quietly disliked the Soviets talked about Uncle Mikelis with a kind of pride.

He'd done some research and discovered that the uncle whom he'd never known but about whom he'd heard so much had been sent to the death camps in the Stalinist era.

That had started to change the relationship between Janis and his idol. Janis had begun to really think for himself. As soon as he did, the image of Julijis not only faded, it turned into something death-like and hateful.

Janis started to read forbidden books on Latvian history, and in reaction he developed a dislike for using the Russian language, which they had to learn in school. He dropped out of organizations like the Young Pioneers and instead spent hours talking to people who had known and remembered the days of independence.

The whole facade of respectability collapsed. There was no way to overtly show the rage he felt after he learned about his country's—and his uncle's—destruction at the hands of the Soviets. There was no protest movement that would be tolerated by the officials. The pain and anger festered inside him.

He had only one real outlet: music. That saved his life. He convinced his family and the school authorities to allow him to concentrate on his natural talent for guitar and piano, and he won a coveted entry into the Riga Conservatory of Music. The idea of joining Julijis at the university faded away into a forgotten dream. In a constricting state, the arts were almost the only means of pushing against the limitations. As the Soviet Union thawed its restrictions, the artistic community—especially in places like Riga—pushed that much harder.

That prompted Janis to form his own contemporary musical group out of the nucleus of a classical ensemble. When things loosened up even more, he established the current rock band, the Teutonic Knights, the center of Janis's current life.

The realization of this truth made Janis learn to hate Julijis and everything he stood for. The feeling was mutual. The former fraternal bond between the two young men had turned into venom and mutual suspicion.

Across the plaza, Julijis pushed and shoved against the would-be demonstrators, none of whom were a match for the strong muscles that filled the drab olive of his uniform. A real hero of a bully with the feeble and the old, Janis thought contemptuously.

Janis saw Julijis's face distorting as he shouted words Janis couldn't hear into the ears of one old woman. She stood her ground as well as she could, staring Julijis in the face as she recoiled from his verbal attack and shrank at the threatening posture he took.

"Isn't that your old friend?" Koren asked.

"Yeah," Janis said, watching as Julijis grabbed the cloth banner the old woman held and yanked it from her hands. Even then she tried desperately to hold it up for all to see.

"Bastard," Janis said quietly, almost softly. "He wishes Joseph Stalin was still in Moscow. Then he could just bat the old woman around and be done with it. Now he actually has to go through procedure in order to get her into a cell where he can do the same thing out of sight."

"Janis!" Koren exclaimed as she quickly looked around at the crowd to see who might have overheard him. "It's one thing for you to test the authorities on the stage with your music, but you can't be going out and protecting demonstrators on the streets of Riga as though you were one of the old fools yourself!"

Confident that no one had paid attention, and wanting to distract Janis from his intent staring at the group of protesters, Koren put a hand on his and squeezed slightly.

"They will be okay," she reassured him. She worried when Janis got in this mood of his. For the past three years, she'd listened to his talking and ranting and raving. It was all masculine posturing, she was sure of it. He was only twenty, barely out of his teens, and certainly powerless to challenge the power of the socialist state.

"You know, they must be crazy to do this," Koren said, hoping to soothe him. "They won't be hurt. That isn't done anymore. They'll just be taken for observation in a hospital—"

Janis yanked his hand from Koren's grasp and turned to look at her with a sudden violence of his own. "There's no difference between a nice hospital of today and a bad prison a few years ago! Those old people will be mistreated, and they'll be kept there until..."

His voice trailed off as he watched the two militiamen follow Julijis's orders and begin to herd the protesters away. Janis looked around and saw with disgust that the other onlookers had gone back to their conversations and their coffees, secretly relieved that the upsetting protest had been so efficiently squelched in a way that wouldn't involve them.

But there will always be protests, Janis thought to himself, silently arguing with the passivity of his fellow countrymen.

"Janis, come on," Koren said quickly, taking advantage of his sudden preoccupation. "It's time for the rehearsal. Besides, you said you wanted to catch the broadcast from Helsinki, the one with Bruce Springsteen, tonight. We'll miss it if we don't move quickly. Come on!"

Janis stood up and stretched his tall body. No one paid attention to him. His loose clothing hid the strength of the muscles he had been resolutely building for years in his makeshift basement gymnasium.

Those who noticed him only saw the unconventional appearance sported by many young people. That was fine by him. It was part of a well-thought-out plan, and it looked as though it was working perfectly. He wanted to give the impression of a harmless musician.

"Okay, okay," he said when he'd relaxed his body, "let's go and do the number again. Maybe we can get Andrievs to play a guitar the way it was meant to be played for a change, instead of making it sound like a percussion instrument."

Putting his hands in his pockets nonchalantly, Janis seemed to search for something he couldn't find.

"Damn it," he said, "I forgot something back at my apartment. Let me meet you at rehearsal. I'll only be a few minutes."

Koren eyed him suspiciously, as though she didn't believe him at all. Then the uncertainty on her face mingled with a suggestive look. Janis could read her mind, and her erotic thoughts made him smirk with pleasure.

"No. We have no time for that. If you come back to my place with me now we'll never make it to rehearsal. You go on. The others will be upset if one of us doesn't show up on time. Tell them that I've just forgotten something and that I'll be there quickly."

He leaned over and planted a soft kiss on her cheek. It brought out a bright blush on the young woman's beautiful complexion, and she gave in. "All right. But don't be long."

Janis ran across Knighthood Square toward the waterfront. He knew that Koren would be watching, but that was no problem. His apartment was on the route he wanted to take anyway.

Once he was on the side streets and out of Koren's sight, he took a sharp turn off the usual path. Janis made quick time as he scurried through the alleyways in the old part of the city near the banks of the Daugava River.

He arrived just in time. He'd suspected that Koren was right and that the demonstrators would be taken to a hospital. This one was the Riga Revolutionary Psychiatric Institute, where the malcontents would be treated for their antisocial behavior.

Janis stopped underneath an overhang that cast a deep shadow over the narrow street and waited. He willed his chest to stop heaving from the exertion of his run, worried that his gasping breaths would give away his presence.

The noises of the city were off in the distance, and the street was quiet, deserted. Then there came the echoing sound of boots marching on pavement and quickly spoken angry words that Janis could hear as the group moved closer. The footfalls stopped, apparently just around the corner.

"There is no need to push her!" one man complained in a loud voice. "We're going peacefully. We—"

"Enough of that!" another voice answered. "We'll show you how peacefully you're going to do what we say once you're inside."

Janis recognized Julijis's voice, and a special hatred burned inside him. He understood that emotion now. If Julijis were simply another Latvian who'd sold out to the Russians it would be bad enough, but this was worse. His friend, his surrogate brother, had turned into the scum of a traitor. Even now, as a young man, Janis couldn't forgive Julijis for his years of posturing for the impressionable younger man. Nor could Janis forgive himself for having bought the act.

This would finally be the time for some repayment, Janis thought to himself. Silently he removed his leather belt, one he'd carefully chosen for its thickness and for its heavy metal buckle. He wrapped the leather around his fist in a way that left the metal hanging loose about fifteen inches from his hand. It was, he'd come to learn, a lethal weapon.

"Take them in. I need to go to headquarters and do the damn paperwork," Julijis was saying to someone now. "Once they're admitted, tell the doctors that they're not to be released without permission from me. And they shouldn't bother asking for it for at least three months."

"Sir!" a soldier answered smartly.

Just then the stomping of boots began again, but one set was moving off in the opposite direction. Janis slunk even farther back under a darkened doorway and waited, bitter because this wasn't going to be his time of confrontation with Julijis after all. Still, he had a chance to act, and that in itself was cause for celebration.

He hefted the heavy metal on the buckle and waited.

If the soldiers had been looking for anyone, they would have seen him easily. They expected no real opposition, and their attention was on the old people, who were becoming more agitated as they got closer to the institute. Janis's dark hair and dark clothes were enough camouflage to give him the seconds of surprise that he needed for this.

He let the small group pass him. One of the soldiers was in front, the other brought up the rear. As soon as the second militiaman had come parallel with him, Janis swung the belt buckle up and backward and then lunged forward, using the heavy metal buckle as a bludgeon.

The sound of steel cracking against skull was sickening. The militiaman never uttered a word. He was dead seconds after the sharp edge of the buckle cut deep into his brain.

The solder fell forward, and Janis yanked back on his belt, trying to pull it free to prepare for the other attack. Nobody had noticed anything amiss, but now he had to regain his primitive weapon. The problem was the buckle, which was embedded in the man's head and wouldn't come free.

Janis dropped the belt and grabbed the man's rifle. It was the AK-47 automatic used by Soviet troops. Like other former Young Pioneers, Janis had had some training in its use. He felt the familiar weight in his hands and automatically lifted it to aim it at the remaining guard.

Suddenly he realized that it would be suicidal. The loud noise of automatic fire in the quiet residential neighborhood would bring dozens of people out and alert the police and militia.

He couldn't fire the gun, but that didn't mean he couldn't use it. Janis hefted the gun by its bore and rushed forward, elbowing past the old lady who had argued with Julijis back at the plaza. She almost screamed in surprise. She hadn't witnessed what had been going on behind her and had been thinking that this was the second guard, bent on doing her even more harm.

Instead, a strange young man with outlandish clothes hurtled toward the second guard. The woman instinctively understood that this new man was on her side, and she clamped her hand over her mouth to stifle a cry of shock.

Janis swung the AK-47 just as the soldier turned. The side of the rifle butt hit the militiaman squarely in the temple. Dropping his own gun on the ground, the man clutched the sides of his head. Another blow to the other side of his head followed, so hard that the protection of his hands was useless.

Blood began to spurt out the man's nose. It came in gushes, even as he fell forward and his forehead hit the pavement with a sickening thud. This was no time to take chances. Janis took the rifle and once more slammed it down on the uniformed body, making sure that the savage blow broke the man's neck.

"Quick, get out. And hide, for God's sake. They'll be looking for you on the streets. Go to the countryside if you can, stay away from the center of the city for as long as possible. Hopefully the other one won't remember you that well."

Janis had whispered his frantic orders to the protesters as he picked up the second guard's AK-47. The automatic rifles would come in handy someday, along with the other supplies he had been hoarding for years.

They stood frozen in fear and disbelief. The young man was telling them to run, but they had come to protest. They weren't about to run away when their point was the honor of Latvia.

They watched indecisively as Janis dashed back to the dead body of the first guard. In a desperate hurry, Janis put his booted foot on the cadaver's back and reached for the leather of the belt. He yanked with great force and freed the buckle. When the metal came out, it left a deep gash that oozed dark red blood.

"Go on!" Janis insisted. "You accomplished what you wanted, and we'll all remember, but we have to live to tell it again another day. You must get out."

Janis didn't have any more time to help, but they had gotten his message and knew without a doubt that he was one of them. They began to rush away as fast as they could, while searching their minds for a place to hide until they could reappear again.

Janis wrapped the two heavy Russian rifles in his jacket and started in the other direction, mentally mapping a route to his apartment that would keep him as far away from other people as possible. As valuable as the AK-47s were, they couldn't be easily explained in the hands of a civilian.

2

"Damn it, Nile, where have you been?" A frustrated Walker Jessup stood beside an enormous stretch limousine outside the Plaza Hotel at the southeast corner of Central Park.

"Walking," Barrabas said as he moved toward the open door of the limousine and climbed in.

Jessup was fuming, and the clouds of smoke he sent billowing from his twenty-dollar cigar seemed to be coming from the hot burning of his emotions. There wasn't anything else he could do but puff away. It wasn't as though he were a man who could afford to pick a fight with Nile Barrabas.

There was the physical deterrent. Nile was a very tall man, but his skeleton was covered by an awesome mass of well-toned, well-trained muscle that he moved with a leonine grace. He'd been able to maneuver his way into the rear of the limo with the agility of a much younger man. Walker Jessup, on the other hand, was almost grotesquely overweight. His belly was so substantially rounded that he could barely see his feet these days. The love of good food that had always been his weakness had become a near-obsession in the past couple of years, and he was also older than Barrabas. He was in no physical condition to challenge the leader of the Soldiers of Barrabas.

That was another reason Jessup was going to have to take whatever Barrabas handed out. Nile's team of crack mercenaries had become Jessup's meal ticket.

Jessup had been known as the "Fixer" since his days at the CIA. Always the one to know the right man for the right job, the right source for the best information, the location of the most sensitive documents, he was usually called as a last resort, for tasks that simply had to be accomplished. Jessup was almost indispensable: he made all the introductions, and lubricated intelligence agencies' constant need for information.

But nothing had worked so well as his latest setup. There was a network in Washington made up of the most powerful people on Capitol Hill, the White House staff and the heads of the country's spy agencies. They had decided that sometimes democracy had to be sidestepped, whether for reasons of security or because swift action allowed no recourse to more legal ways.

The United States simply had to have a way to act without interference and with immediate response when necessary. There had to be some people who were capable of feats of heroism when the need arose.

Jessup had seen it all coming and had talked to some of the major players in the world of Washington's inner circles, the real seats of power. What if there were a team put together by one of the country's greatest military heroes, a man incredibly well trained and educated and with almost superhuman courage? What if such a force—backed with the latest American technology and given the covert help of a very few American agencies when it was necessary—were available for hire on a case-by-case basis?

How much would it be worth?

The answer was lots. Jessup had loved the sound of the single word. It would be worth a whole lot of money to the government, which had ways of hiding the expenditures easily enough. That was when Jessup had gotten in touch with Nile Barrabas and asked him to pull together a team. The team acquired the name Soldiers of Barrabas, or SOBs for short. They would be paid very very handsomely indeed to remain at the ready and available for hire.

The particular members of the team evolved over a matter of time, but the membership was pretty well set now. What was more set was the leadership—just one person, just Nile Barrabas. Without him there would be no team, and Walker Jessup knew it. Without the SOBs there would be no huge fees. Without the huge fees there would be no commissions. Without the commissions Walker Jessup would be a poor man. That would not do.

His finder's fee for the services of the group of combat veterans had become increasingly important to Jessup to support a life-style that included the ability to afford exorbitantly expensive gourmet meals.

Without the SOBs there would be no dinners at Maxim's.

Finally Jessup had hit upon a soothing topic. There was always dinner at one of the world's premier restaurants to think about. His mouth filled with saliva at the very idea, and the daydreams of his upcoming meal crowded out the minor annoyance of Nile Barrabas being late for what was really a relatively minor appointment.

A smile appeared on Jessup's face as he threw away the butt of his expensive cigar and climbed awkwardly after Barrabas into the limousine. When Jessup slammed the door, the chauffeur immediately pulled the huge automobile out of its parking space and headed north through Central Park, aiming for Connecticut.

Somebody spoke up from the corner of one of the plush seats. "Nile, I'm so excited I can't begin to tell you. I mean, I want you to know that I feel as though I'm anticipating a date with a voluptuous starlet of my dreams."

Barrabas looked over at the slightly built man who had been waiting in the car and smiled. Nate Beck was the most unlikely person to be a member of the SOBs, and he probably did mean just what he'd said. The subject of the event he looked forward to was capable of getting him carried away. Beck took the idea of being a "computer nerd" to new extremes. He lived for his megabytes and played his computer keyboard with all the passion that a great pianist saved for his own.

Women? Beck loved women. Nile knew that. But the computer specialist had had his problems with the opposite sex, most specifically with his ex-wife, a woman whose passion for spending money had been as great as Beck's own thirst for expansion slots. Beck had become wary of women, especially those who had any intention of making long-term claims on him.

"Calm down, Nate," Barrabas said as he comfortably stretched out his legs. "This is just a trade show."

"Just a trade show!" Beck seemed to be in pain as he protested that remark, as though his mother had just been insulted. "Nile, this is one of the most important events in American technological evolution! This is the first time we're really going to see the massive applications of computer science to everyday life."

"Dangerous," Walker Jessup spouted from his own side of the car. "Letting all this stuff loose in the world. It's just greedy of the manufacturers, wanting to try and make sure they have at least a little bit of the money the Japanese are making. Just grandstanding, that's all, to make sure they don't lose out on the high-tech market."

"It's only a little true," Beck admitted softly. "Sure, the United States is in danger of falling behind the Japanese in some ways, but our abilities haven't really been tested yet. This show today—"

"Is going to tell too much," Jessup said, interrupting him. He was scowling. The conversation was interfering with his dreams of veal pâté and his anticipation of champagne bubbles. "That's the truth of it.

"The problem with selling this kind of technology is that the buyer has to be told just what the goods are. It's bad enough that our Freedom of Information Act opens up many files that would normally be kept in sensitive secrecy and that we already have such gaps in our intelligence. For God's sake! Our children know all about the most top-secret project in our Air Force!"

Now Jessup was back to his fuming. He reached inside his suit jacket and pulled out another of his cigars. It wasn't so much that he needed the tobacco; he felt compelled to make his point dramatic with a cloud of smoke.

He was talking about the Stealth bomber, Barrabas surmised. The treasured project of the Air Force was a supersonic jet bomber made of materials that had been specially formulated to avoid detection by even the most modern radar. While congressmen and Department of Defense officials spoke in hushed tones about the secret weapon, one of the largest toy manufacturers in the country had gone through public records. By using random pieces of data and putting together hints of design features from press reports, they had figured out precisely the design of the plane. Suddenly, instead of dealing with a hush-hush project, the head honchos of the United States were dealing with a plastic model that was shipped in time for the Christmas selling season, to everyone's great chagrin.

Nate sank back into the seat of the limo and stayed silent. Even if Walker Jessup was going to stink up the car with his obnoxious cigar and at the same time attempt to put a damper on Beck's enthusiasm, Nate couldn't hold back the thrill he felt. The North American Air and Space Technological Fair had all the makings of a kid's day at the circus to him.

While the two men sitting on either side of him reverted into their private worlds, Nile Barrabas stared straight ahead as the chauffeur pulled onto the New England Thruway and continued to travel north. All Barrabas cared about concerning this little outing was that the senator was going to be there and had asked for his presence.

That only meant one thing: there was a job in the offing. He'd have to call together his team and take them out into the field. There was a kind of excitement to it for Nile, but there was also the fact that as a leader he was always risking the safety of his followers—a far greater responsibility than simply having to look out for himself.

In the military orders are orders, and officers receive them from above and pass them on to obedient soldiers. But when you're a private operative you have to look at every assignment and wonder if it's really worth the risk—not to you, to your troops.

What did the senator have up his sleeve this time? Nile wondered. And why the unusual procedure of meeting in Connecticut?

BRADLEY INTERNATIONAL AIRPORT serves both Hartford, Connecticut, and Springfield, Massachusetts. It was one of the enormous air bases made available to civilian use after their military usefulness was over. Once the home base for many American Air Force bomber groups, Bradley was now the center of air transportation for much of the area between Boston and New York.

It was also home for the first North American Air and Space Technological Fair, which was already showing signs of becoming one of the great international arms bazaars.

The three men made a strange trio as they strode up and down the lines of aeronautical wonders displayed on the airport's side runways. At the center of the group was Nile Barrabas, quiet, studying the matériel in front of them carefully. His obvious strength and the stark white streaks in his thick hair made the big man all the more noticeable among the crowds of men and women.

While Barrabas was the one to draw notice to his group, the two men on either side of him made sure that the little entourage stayed the center of attention.

Nate Beck, a quick-witted, excitable guy, seemed to be wired. He gestured with the abandon of an orchestra conductor, then took off at a trot for some display he'd just spotted with the passion of a rock groupie beholding the star of his dreams.

Jessup's lumbering gait and statuelike mass when he anchored himself before any exhibit with a sour expression garnered him many a second glance.

The runway was lined with the latest jet fighter offerings from Boeing, Lockheed and the rest of the American industry's largest aerospace corporations. The display was beautiful, and that wasn't only Nate Beck's opinion. Everyone who wandered through the show shared the same point of view; the prototypes of aircraft in development had an amazing grace to them. For the general public it was awesome to realize there was still the possibility of something looking futuristic in the age of the Concorde and automated factories. Some of the aircraft had been developed from ideas from the space program or the Strategic Defense Initiative and seemed to be products of the best creative minds of Hollywood.

What was on display was the cutting edge, products that for the most part had just been released for foreign sale by the Department of Defense, which had declared them valuable for allies' consumption for peaceful use, even if some of them could be applied to military uses.

Almost all the products on sale were items that would require an "end use permit" from the Department of Trade. The purchasers would have to agree that the goods wouldn't be reexported to a different market, one where the U.S. government had no say about the final applications of the technology.

That had become a growing problem as America's firms had stretched their horizons, desperately looking for new export markets. Benign-appearing hardware, sold to Norway and Japan for domestic use, had found its way into Russia. The problem was immense because the simple mechanisms involved, which had to do with high-tech propellers for seagoing vessels, contained some of the world's most important submarine technology.

The one place the U.S. had maintained its superiority over the Russians on a consistent basis was in underwater warfare, and now that edge was gone. The Russians had simply gone into the marketplace and purchased the most advanced designs and knowledge. They hadn't even had to work for it.

"Come on, Nile, let's go inside, that's where the real action is!" Nate Beck suggested to Barrabas in a frenzy of enthusiasm. Nile smiled with amusement at his friend's excitement and let himself be guided in the direction of one of the hangars where the electronics portion of the show was displayed.

"Damn fool cowboys!" Walker Jessup scowled in an increasingly foul mood as he followed the SOBs across the tarmac. "Acting like schoolboys at a *Play-*

boy convention instead of soldiers going about their work.''

The mutters had no effect on the two SOBs, and Jessup had no choice but to try to keep up with them. The other two men had quickened their pace, and Jessup was able to match it for a while, but he eventually had to drop back out of sheer embarrassment about the way his flesh heaved when he moved fast.

The August heat didn't help any. The limousine's air conditioning had sheltered him from the brutal summer sun on their drive up from New York City, but in the open the temperature was in the nineties, and the weather was getting to him. He felt slippery with sweat by the time he found some relief in the shade of the hangar. He pulled out his handkerchief and began to dab up the perspiration from his glistening face.

He could remember the days during the Korean War when he had been a soldier himself and in top shape. His thoughts drifted fondly to this youthful and dapper image. He could have beaten anybody at games of who-lasts-longer. Now he could only count on slackening muscles, he thought as his eyes roved around idly.

But his sight wasn't going to fail him, at least. Jessup put his limp handkerchief back into his pocket, his manner suddenly deliberate. His eyes were focused on one particular man who was walking through the electronics display. Walker Jessup stopped playing the part of an irate fat man, and a keen look appeared in his eyes as he recognized Nikoli Geogi.

What the hell was the man doing there?

Jessup studied Geogi intently. This was really his own strength, to know things, sum up people and recognize danger when it might not be apparent to anyone else.

Nikoli Geogi was one of the top operatives of the Soviet spy network. He was camouflaged as a civilian air transport specialist at the Soviet embassy in Washington. That was daring of the Soviets, who usually tried to pretend their operatives were cultural attachés or something equally benign. Geogi got red-carpet treatment in his actual position, though. After all, civilian air transport was the largest single source of export income the United States earned these days.

The Japanese had bested the USA in radios and microwaves, the Germans edged ahead in the world's car market, the French leaped ahead of America in rail transport, but no one had really challenged the might of the U.S. aircraft industry. The factories turning out 747s in Seattle and DC-9s in St. Louis and all of the other industrial giants of the air were the most solid industrial advantage the country had.

The net result was that the Department of Commerce and other Washington bureaucracies that only studied the bottom line of the trade deficit and other markers of economic health loved everyone who said they wanted to buy airplanes, even the Russians.

Nikoli Geogi didn't need an assumed name to wander through the show: he was welcome. The Russian civilian air fleet was tired, and internal demand for fast, efficient transport was booming. Jessup knew full well that any one of the exhibitors would have gotten down on their knees and begged to get Geogi's business. There was an unlimited number of airplanes to be sold if the Soviets would condescend to buying American products.

National pride had blocked the Russians up till now, but the horizons of trade were due to open up as the demand for consumer goods and better services became a higher priority in the Soviet Union.

The spy didn't need a deep cover, Jessup snorted to himself silently, because the greed of American business made it willing to rip open its heart for him. Buy our secrets! Please! That was their message to the man.

Jessup watched Geogi walking through the displays and experienced a deep desire to know just what the Russian was looking at. Jessup didn't understand the language of the technological marketplace, and he didn't want to. He suddenly yearned even more for those days during the Korean War, not only for the trim body he'd had but for the simplicity of warfare then.

Those had been days when men had faced one another with nothing more than their rifles and simple-to-understand and simple-to-operate artillery. There were no laser beams to bring confusion, no microchips to tell a real human male where to go, no optical disk systems to store the entire arms inventory of the Army on one silvery thing looking like a 45 RPM record.

Men had done the fighting then for what they believed in. Now there were machines doing the battles and planning the strategy. Jessup looked around the hall once more and shook his head in disbelief. Who would ever have thought that, having come across a Russian spy, Walker Jessup would have to go and ask someone's help to find out what the damned ass was spying on?

Modern times, indeed!

He padded off to the right, following the lead of Nile Barrabas, whose silvery hair he could make out at a distance. Jessup forgot his dignity and began to do the closest thing to a jog that he could imagine, allowing his belly to jiggle along with him, making him feel as though he were in danger of becoming a beach ball, one that risked bouncing once with too much gusto, lifting him up into the air.

"Hey! Barrabas! Nile! Hold on!"

Everyone turned to see Walker yelling as he struggled up the aisle toward the white-haired warrior. The nice politeness of multimillion-dollar deals was being broken by the loud yells. It was no way to run a corporation!

"Hold it, Nate," Nile said as he heard Jessup's call. Nate Beck had just led Barrabas into a display for a new laser sighting system that, while developed for use on the battlefield, could have important applications in civilian airports. It had been designed to allow a tank, say, to use the technology to guide its fire with unerring aim. The same science could guide a jetliner to a pinpoint landing in the worst weather conditions.

Beck had just begun to explain all that to the leader of the SOBs when Barrabas had asked him to slow it down.

"You two, I swear!" Jessup had caught up with the two soldiers and was once again dragging out his handkerchief to wipe his brow. "You just have no sense of—"

Jessup's gasping breath didn't let him finish the sentence. It didn't do his mood any good to see that his two companions weren't sweating at all. Without meaning to, they had both subconsciously dressed as though they were in uniform and had a crisp military look about them. They each had on sharply pressed chino slacks and highly polished cordovan loafers. Their shirts differed only in the color of the light cotton fabric. Nile's was a light olive drab, while Nate's was white. Still, the cut was similar—down to the epaulets on the shoulders.

"What's wrong? Are you sick?" Beck asked.

It infuriated Jessup to have his discomfort labeled that way. It was normal to perspire in the heat and to catch one's breath after running. Was it really fair to blame Jessup just because these two Rambos kept their bodies in superhuman condition and therefore didn't have to go through what more ordinary mortals did. Disgusted, Walker realized Barrabas and Beck looked impeccably fresh and that even their shirts didn't cling to them. Inhumanly cool, that was what they were.

"I just thought you two might be willing to do some work instead of pretending that this place was simply a big-time toy warehouse," Jessup said caustically.

"He must be hungry," Barrabas said softly to Beck.

That was unfair, though, Jessup admitted to himself, it was true. As soon as he'd heard Barrabas's words, he felt an emotional tug toward fulfilling his true love, good food. But there was work to be done, and Jessup wasn't going to be diverted, even by that.

"I need you two. We have a very special friend here, and I have to understand what he's up to. Come on, follow me." Jessup swiveled around and began to walk back down the aisles with the others behind him. The best part of the new development was that he could set the pace. Thank God! And while he was certainly concerned about catching up with Nikoli, that didn't mean he needed to break any track records.

The high ceiling of the old hangar made for weird acoustics, with distorted echoes reverberating throughout the hall. The structure had originally been built in the 1940s as part of the home effort against the Germans, and there was a faint art deco quality to the hangar because of the date of construction. All the old parts of the building were in sharp contrast to the exhibits.

The major corporations had invested a lot of money and effort in their high-tech displays. Videos highlighted special features of the products and offered simulations of the new technology in action. As the three men headed for their goal, they passed the major corporate enclaves. The very names shouted the height of American science: Raytheon, Northrop, on and on the list went.

Jessup's eyes honed in on his target. Nikoli Geogi was still standing before the booth of Continental Air Systems Ltd., where Jessup had last spotted him.

Stopping short just before the entrance to the Continental booth, Jessup asked, "Remember him, Nile?" without taking his eyes off the Russian.

Nile Barrabas studied Nikoli Geogi for a moment before pursing his lips in a silent whistle of surprise. "That son of a bitch" was all the white-haired man said, and his soft voice actually conveyed more anger and hatred than any theatrical grandstanding someone else might have resorted to. Nile Barrabas obviously did know Nikoli Geogi, and he hated him.

Geogi was chatting amiably with a Continental sales representative. The Russian was dressed in what looked to be the latest London men's fashion. His three-piece suit was formal, but there was a rakish cut to it, and clearly he could wear such clothes well.

Nikoli was about Nile's age, in his early forties. He was balding but doing it quite well, not trying to be silly in the way he combed what was left of his hair. He'd actually had it trimmed to a quarter-inch of bristle, making himself look all the more masculine and military. The discreet hint of purple and orange in his tie was another clue to his interest in looking good, and so was the contrasting color of the collar on his dress shirt.

The Continental employee he was talking to was certainly properly impressed, especially by that name tag of Geogi's. He was fawning all over the Russian.

At that level of commerce, where a deal might mean hundreds of millions of dollars, no one was crass enough to bring out an order book and pin a potential customer on the spot. These people were geared to long-term selling, for the most part. An opening was all that could be expected from the show, a first chance to fix someone's interest in a product. Deals would be made, and the sums would be enough to spin any head on Wall Street, but almost all of them were the end result of many months' and perhaps years' worth of work.

That didn't mean a big potential customer wasn't welcomed as he perused the aisles, and Nikoli Geogi was acting like the biggest of the big. He was warm and friendly, smiling graciously at the sales rep and listening carefully to the rap he was getting.

"What's he looking at, Beck? Go in there and find out. If that man's after something in our arsenal, we need to discover what it is and why he wants it."

Nate nodded after Jessup had given his orders. The small man walked calmly into the Continental Air Systems Ltd. booth and began to look around.

"You knew damned well I'd remember him," Barrabas said in a tight-lipped way as soon as Nate had left. "Don't ever play those games with me again."

Jessup looked over at Nile and saw him staring with angry intent at the Russian. "You're enough of a professional to be over that," he said calmly.

Nile turned a chilling gaze on Jessup. "No one ever gets over anything like that and still gets to call himself a human being."

"Did you love her?" Jessup asked quietly, almost respectfully. "Did you really?"

Pain wasn't an expression that crossed Nile Barrabas's face very often, but it was discernible in his features at that moment. He didn't answer the question. He simply stood there, immersed in his memories.

He'd been involved with a woman named Sophia in Istanbul more than ten years previously. She had been beautiful, with the peculiar beauty of those whose actual nationality is lost in the cross-fertilization of continents and races. There had been hints of Africa in her dusky skin and an Oriental cast to her eyes. Her sharp blue eyes had shone from the dark olive skin around them. Her long, luxuriously thick black hair had seemed to come from the environs of the Aegean. All the world, it had often seemed, had contributed to her incredible looks.

She was one of the few women who had ever made it into Nile Barrabas's soul. There had been a way about her that had made him discover his own boyishness. He could remember even now the blush that had crept over him when he'd brought her flowers—and he'd done it with every date.

Nikoli Geogi had been attached to the Soviet consulate in Istanbul then. The woman had been one of his operatives. Nile hadn't known that; he couldn't have. But one night he'd approached the house where she lived just as the Turkish military police were leaving, with her in tow.

He had never given up a single secret and couldn't remember any time she'd asked him leading questions. There hadn't been an instance when their time together hadn't been sacred between them.

In all probability the two of them had had a chance encounter. They'd met at a bar in one of the big downtown hotels and hit it off right away. They didn't really exchange much information about themselves, but just gloried in each other. The usual agenda didn't evolve, and nothing indicated that she wanted anything from him but his body and his affections—which he'd granted freely. The fact that they were both in Istanbul on ''business'' was almost assuredly a coincidence.

But it was a coincidence that Nile Barrabas had never gotten over, and it had changed the way he looked at an experienced woman ever since. Even now, with his one ongoing relationship, Barrabas withdrew at times, and that woman in Istanbul was the strong force coming between him and anyone else.

Barrabas had always blamed Nikoli Geogi for it all. He'd followed the investigation and the trial as carefully as he could. Once the ring of spies had been broken, Geogi had been hurried out of the country on the strength of his diplomatic passport to make sure there wasn't undue embarrassment for his masters back in Moscow.

The man himself hadn't been present for the public humiliation that Sophia had undergone, but he had caused it. He'd taken a woman who had begun her life in the world's most forgotten and forgettable refugee camps, and he'd offered her money and security. All for a few extra favors to a select few who might tell her a few extra details about NATO's defensive plans.

That had begun it all. Nile wanted to believe, he had a deep-down need to believe that the coincidence of their meeting and the intensity of their feelings had had to do only with themselves, not with anything that involved global politics.

But he would never really know.

The possibility that she hadn't loved him but had set him up had plagued him ever since. Once burned, he had never approached that particular fire again. He needed more time with women now. He needed history with them to know that they wanted him for himself. There were no more simple escapist romances in Nile's life. Sophia had made sure of that.

The last time he'd seen her had been on the day of her sentencing. He'd watched as she pleaded her case and swore that she was a mere cipher in the whole operation, only a woman in need who had done what she must in order to survive. Nile had studied her and felt his whole self being pulled apart. Half of him believed her and believed her passionately. That part of him wanted to rescue her. He remembered the sensations he'd experienced in the courtroom, how he'd wanted to pull a gun and start shooting, to get her out of the clutches of the impossibly cruel Turkish justice system. He knew damned well what Turkish jails were like, and it certainly appeared that Sophia would spend the rest of her life inside the walls of one of them.

The other half of him, though, wanted her to get all she had coming. That half was forced to consider the possibility that everything between them had been a sham. If so, then the performance in front of the tribunal was just another stage part for the lady, just another role like the one she'd played in bed with him.

Nile lived with that conflict for five years. Then it was resolved for him when he read a report in the *International Herald-Tribune* while sitting at a Paris coffee shop. The article reported a daring commando raid on a Turkish prison. The Turks had announced that some leaders of the Kurdish separatist movement had been freed by their compatriots, and all the press was buying the line. Nile read the dispatch carefully and he'd discovered one thing wrong with the whole thing: Sophia had been one of the people who'd been sprung in the breakout. No matter how international her background, there was no connection between her and the Kurds, a nomadic people whose homeland was divided between Turkey, Iran and Iraq and who fought all three governments with equal fervor.

When eventually the Kurds were recaptured, Sophia was still at large. Barrabas had known then without a doubt that Nikoli Geogi had been behind the operation. He'd gone back to do what any good spymaster must do: free his runner after she'd been caught. The Kurds were a blind for the public's consumption.

More than any court ruling, that had proved Sophia had been guilty as accused, and Barrabas knew she must have been after him for something more than his love. No one that important to the Soviets spends any time on a simple fling with an American mercenary. If freeing her was worth risking an international incident, which was possible with that kind of prison break, then her masters thought her too valuable to ever allow her free time to find a man on her own. She had been directed, and Barrabas had been the target.

It had been the end of Nile's dream, and the scars on his memory still hurt.

Nikoli Geogi was the source of all that pain.

3

The scene played over and over again in Nile's mind.

He had been carrying a dozen red roses up the narrow street in Istanbul. He'd whistled an old love song, full of romance and the kinds of emotions that only adolescents experience and not grown men.

But he was feeling them. His step was jaunty and carefree.

He turned the familiar corner. The beautiful hybrid roses in his hand had no odor, but his nostrils were full of smells. He was anticipating the sweetness of Sophia. There was her perfume, of course, but he was tantalized more by her own natural scent, something that reminded him of a precious spice and brought out images of the East and exotic locales.

The street looked the same as it always did. Her house, with its bright doorway, was midway down the block, and Nile sped up his pace, almost overcome by a need to hold her.

Suddenly Sophia's door burst open, and she was shoved through it, her arms firmly in the grasp of two huge men.

Nile threw down the roses. Without hesitation he moved quickly toward the woman who was in such obvious danger.

Sophia was quickly moved away from the door. Two more men appeared from behind, and the group started to move away from the house.

Adrenaline surged through Nile's body, removing considerations of danger and any thought of his own safety. The pair who'd come last already had their backs to him. That was a mistake that allowed Nile to call on his martial arts training.

He took a running leap toward them. His body was propelled up into the air, feetfirst, and his steel-toed boots struck each of the Turks full in the back of the neck. As the metal-reinforced boots crushed their vertebrae, their nervous systems were dealt a fatal blow, and they crumpled to the ground.

Nile landed squarely on their backs. The ones holding his beloved Sophia had barely enough time to turn to confront their attacker. Nile's well-trained hands sliced through the air toward their vulnerable temples. The blow delivered by the sides of his palms stunned the two men. Nile quickly reared back and delivered jarring jabs to the men's abdomens. They doubled up in pain and shock but had no time to recover as Nile jackknifed his knee to brutally crack his kneecaps against their foreheads. They tumbled backward, falling with such force that their skulls connected sickeningly with the unyielding asphalt.

Then Nile had grabbed Sophia, and the two of them had taken off in a wild sprint to get away—away from the danger, from their pasts, away. . . .

"Nile! Have you heard what I've said at all?" Jessup asked, and gave him a curious look. Then he resumed his pacing around the suite in the Hilton just outside the gates of Bradley Field.

Jessup quickly recapped what he'd said, and something he said jolted Barrabas's memory—the kind of thing that separates fact from fantasy. The four men in the mentally reenacted scene had been wearing Turkish police uniforms. Their leader, Lieutenant Izuturk, had been a friend of his, and they hadn't been abducting Sophia but arresting her.

A further fact was that Nile hadn't fought them. His roses dangling from his hand, he had watched in disbelief and with a sense of betrayal as Izuturk had explained Sophia's role in the Soviet espionage network that had been preying on NATO secrets.

"All right, Jessup," Barrabas said as he stood up from his comfortable chair and walked across the room to the bar. He poured himself a drink. "You and Nate are playing kids' games about all this technology. Let's get to the point before I drift off again."

Barrabas sipped his drink and headed back to his chair, walking past the agitated Nate Beck, who was perched on the edge of the couch.

"Look, I tell you, that stuff is just dynamite. It's explosive. How can they even think about selling it to the Russians?"

"Profits, dear boy," Jessup said. He'd taken a cue from Nile and walked over to the bar, where he poured himself a draft of bourbon that was much more substantial than Nile's light Scotch and soda. "We're dealing with some very major trade deficits, remember."

"Hell. Doesn't anyone in Washington understand that the one thing we have over the Russians are computers? Look, even with *glasnost* the Soviets restrict copiers, for God's sake. It's a crime for a citizen to own a Xerox or a mimeograph machine in the Eastern bloc! That's how much they have to keep control over the means of communications. We have computers in almost every grade school in the U.S. now—certainly in most high schools—and it's getting harder to get a job out of college if you don't understand a computer keyboard and know your modems from your bytes. But the basic personal computer is at least as dangerous to the Soviets as a Xerox is!

"With the most basic computers you can communicate across great expanses of space through the use of telephone lines with such speed that no one can ever bug you. Infinite numbers of documents can be duplicated in a matter of minutes and distributed at will. You can transport an entire forbidden novel on a simple floppy disk.

"A totalitarian regime can't tolerate personal computers any more than they can tolerate a free press. It's essentially the same thing. That gives us the biggest edge we have for the future, because that means that the Russians can't teach their children the way we teach ours. And that means the Russians can't develop a whole generation of computer-literate kids like we have. We are giving our next generation a chance to become computer programmers, to learn the ways and the ins and outs of the computer and have the opportunity to give us new inventions, new software, new applications."

Beck looked around with indignation and incredulity on his face. "So what are the damn companies doing here? They're selling our edge to the other side! I can't believe it. Sure, there's no question that the product Continental has come up with could be very useful in commercial aviation. But don't you see that it's the same program we use to defend our airspace from attack.''

Shifting uncomfortably in his seat, Jessup turned a mock-stern glance at their lecturer. ''Now, slow down, Nate. Don't leave somebody like me who still isn't so sure about electric typewriters too far behind. Why do you say all that?''

''Because—'' the exasperated Beck took a deep breath to try to control his emotions ''—the function of the air control system that Continental is selling out there on the floor of the fair is essentially the same as our most sophisticated air defense system. The whole point to the Continental system is to track airplanes. Sure, it works when you want to know what planes are in the sky and which ones are at what altitudes, and that sounds totally benign, I know that. It just sounds like, well, traffic control. But the same basic elements to that system can also be utilized to warn of the approach of enemy aircraft—missiles, bombers—and to track them.''

Nate Beck was frustrated by his inability to explain all the technology to laymen. He knew what he was talking about, but he couldn't get the facts out in a way that someone who didn't really know computers could understand. ''I know I can't tell you just the way it works, but to someone like me—''

''Or Nikoli Geogi,'' Nile Barrabas said coldly from his corner seat.

Nate looked over at his boss. ''I don't know who he is, Nile, but if he knows anything about computerized defense systems, he saw what I saw.''

"We'll just make sure he doesn't buy one, then," Barrabas said, looking directly at Walker Jessup.

"Nile, I don't know. I just don't know how we're going to get the senator to agree to this."

Barrabas took a sip of his Scotch. "Maybe the senator doesn't even have to know. Sometimes things just happen to men."

"Forget it, Nile!" Walker Jessup suddenly assumed an uncharacteristically grave expression as he continued talking. "You can't provoke an international incident of those proportions when everything is going so...swell between the Soviets and the administration in power. Don't you dare mess with Moscow-Washington talks."

Barrabas didn't answer but looked out the big picture window of the Hilton, out over the sprawl of suburban Hartford.

Jessup began to pace again. "We just have to wait for the senator to get here. After all, he's been the main opponent to any trade with the Eastern bloc. He'll be the last person in the world who'd want to sell them anything as sophisticated as that Continental product."

THE LEAR JET WAS DESCENDING toward Bradley at just that moment. The senator was sitting in the luxurious private plane and, as he was whenever he was surrounded by the pleasures of the life of the rich and famous, he felt very much at ease.

He enjoyed the comfort of the thickly upholstered chair much more than the limitation of his usual seat, a wheelchair to which he'd been confined for many years. He delighted in the things power had brought him; they still, to some extent, compensated for his disability.

There was also the compensation incarnated in Miss Roseline. "Senator, time to fasten your seat belt," his ever-efficient secretary and majordomo announced with her untiring smile.

The beautiful young woman came and bent over to attach the metal clasp of the belt around the senator's lap. He loved moments such as this and came up with any number of excuses to arrange them and thus afford himself the lovely vistas of her cleavage.

Even if his accident had left him physically impotent, there was still the ability to savor the visual delights of a perfect young woman.

A voice came across the intercom from the cockpit, interrupting the gentle moment just as the senator was wondering if she'd just let him feel those beautiful mounds of hers, just once. "Sir, we should— Bloody hell!"

Miss Roseline stood up suddenly and screamed. "Oh, my God!"

"What is it! What's wrong with you?" Even as he yelled his questions, the senator followed Miss Roseline's line of vision and peered out the window of the jet. There, only a couple of hundred feet away, was the nose of a 747.

The Lear jet suddenly seemed to drop from the sky. Another loud, piercing scream tore through the cabin as her body lifted up from the floor of the plane and was thrown violently against the ceiling. There was another lurch and the young woman came crashing down, slammed against another of the seats, tossed around as though she were a play-doll, and not the kind the senator had been visualizing only seconds before.

Then, as though they'd moved into the eye of a hurricane, the Lear jet leveled off and seemed to be proceeding smoothly, as though nothing had happened.

The pilot's voice came back over the intercom, but with none of his usual calm. The man was clearly shaky himself. "I'm very sorry. Air traffic control at Bradley must have messed up. We nearly got blown out of the sky by that jumbo jet."

"Damn you!" The senator cried out in frustration and from the pain that had cut into his waist as his own body had been forcibly restrained by his seat belt. "Miss Roseline is hurt. Get this thing on the ground and alert the tower to have an ambulance ready."

The intercom voice responded smartly to the tone of authority in the senator's voice. "Yes, sir!"

"And warn Bradley air traffic control that someone's head is going to roll."

The responding "Yes, sir!" sounded different. A paid staff member had heard the anger and the meanness in the threat. When the senator said that heads were going to roll, it usually turned out to be the truth, and one that materialized quickly.

BARRABAS WAS TALKING to the Lear jet's pilot while Nate Beck questioned the senior air traffic controller from the Bradley tower. It was Walker Jessup's problem that he was the one who was speaking to the senator.

The old man's face wasn't attractive under the best of conditions. Age and drink had dried it up, leaving it marked with deep lines that lent an ugly series of contours to his profile. He had never been an imposing figure of a man. Even before the accident that had confined him to his wheelchair, he'd been stoop-shouldered and painfully thin. All those unattractive qualities seemed to be simply magnified by his disability.

"I tell you, Jessup, this is an outrage! A member of the United States Senate nearly murdered in the sky by an American jumbo jet!" The senator turned to the quiet and soft-spoken traffic controller who was still talking to Nate. "What possible excuse do you have?"

The man blanched and looked quickly from the senator to Beck, as though he hoped the SOBs' computer expert could help him out of this horrible spot.

"Sir," the controller finally said, "we're very sorry, but our equipment is out of date. With the Air and Space Technological Fair taking up so much of our tarmac space, we just were strained to our limits. If we'd had the new Continental system we've been begging Congress for—"

"You can have any goddamn system you want! There are hundreds of millions of dollars in a special trust fund for airport improvements. Take it! Take it all if it means I never have to go through anything like that again!"

"But Continental says it hasn't received the requisite number of orders to allow it to go into full production—"

"I'll deal with Continental and you'll deal with installing that damn thing." The senator cut off the civil servant with his acid-tongued reply. "Now, see to Miss Roseline, the poor, dear lady."

Jessup looked at the old politician with awe. He could hardly believe the old scoundrel could use words like "poor, dear lady" and not be struck down by lightning. The expressions didn't seem to be the right kind to come out of his mouth.

But the softly moaning Miss Roseline was being attended to by paramedics who had arrived on the scene just as soon as the plane's doors had opened. Now they were carrying her down the gangway of the Lear jet on a stretcher.

The senator steered his electric wheelchair over to them, nearly knocking over one of the stretcher bearers in the process. "Miss Roseline! Miss Roseline..."

"She'll be all right, sir. Just a little shaken up," one of the men assured the senator. "We're going to take her into the city to have her checked at one of the hospitals. We have your number at the Hilton, and we'll call and let you know how things are as soon as we can."

The paramedics were obviously used to dealing with distraught people of all kinds and weren't about to be intimidated, not even by a United States senator. They efficiently and effectively hustled Miss Roseline into the ambulance and slammed the doors shut.

The senator sat in hostile silence as he watched the vehicle move away with its lights blinking and its siren sounding. He only spun around to address the others after it had turned onto the exit ramp to leave the airport grounds.

"Let's get to this hotel and have a drink. God knows I need one."

Miss Roseline showed up at the Hilton two hours later. Her pleasant and beautiful, if often devious, face was screwed up in anger. Her neck was ensconced in a tight foam brace, forcing her already prominent jaw to point upward even more than she'd been taught to do at Miss Porter's school years ago.

"Are you all right?" the senator demanded when he saw his closest aide standing in the doorway to the suite.

The tired and disheveled Miss Roseline didn't answer until she'd taken a seat in a chair that Nate had quickly abandoned for her. She sat down gingerly, obviously not used to the restrictions of the brace and also very wary from some past experiences with pain caused by quick motion.

"I will live," Miss Roseline said with grand elocution.

"This is a miracle, and one that has nothing to do with the American air traffic system," the senator said. He'd drunk an astounding amount of bourbon during the short time Miss Roseline had been absent.

"They wanted me to stay in the hospital for a week!" Miss Roseline added quickly and disbelievingly. "But I knew you couldn't manage. I had to sign out against doctor's orders."

Everyone in the room felt the weight of that statement of devotion. A major repayment would be collected sometime soon for that melodramatic declaration. The senator seemed to lose his moment of drama when he heard the words, and he suddenly hung his head, much like a punished dog who knew there was still another blow to come from his owner, and soon.

"I am eternally grateful, as I always am," he said, admitting quick and total defeat, then turned to Jessup. "This is the end of your conversation, Walker. All this technological rigmarole you and your fancy mercenaries are giving me is hogwash. We have got to make the American skies safe for civilians like Miss Roseline and me. Continental has the perfect way to do it. There are government funds available down the line, but it'll take time to spring them. I'm going to change my position on the Senate floor and push for release of the Continental system to foreign sales."

The senator held up his hand. "Don't give me any of your tired arguments. There are untold numbers of safeguards in our system of exporting. This thing won't get in the Russians' hands. After all, there must be a guarantee from the receiving country that technological material such as this won't be reexported. That end use document is more than enough to make sure that only friendly countries use this incredible safety measure for civilian purposes."

"Senator, you know damn well that any good smuggler can get around that, and hundreds of them have without any problem in the past. This thing is just too sophisticated—"

The senator wanted none of Jessup's objections and interrupted the other man's speech. "It's done, Walker. That's all there is to it. We have to start to use foreign investments to develop this kind of thing. We've underwritten the rest of the world for years, decades, and the United States simply can't afford it any longer. We can't put an American flag on every damn ship in the world and make believe we can pay for its protection ourselves. I'm the last person in the world to give away our information to the Russkies, and you know it. I won't allow that. But foreign investments in the form of advance orders for this air traffic control system will help our economy. Damn liberals have tied up these moneys as tight as their grandmothers' purse strings. It'll take time to free them up.

"You heard the Continental reps we had in here. They don't have enough of their own cash to start up actual production. The more orders they can get, the more they can spread out the development costs. They can get going on a profitable basis right away if they can land those foreign orders, pay for their overhead, and by the time we're ready for domestic orders, much of the start-up expenses will have been covered.

"We need new approaches to marketing our technology." The senator paused to drain the rest of his tall glass of bourbon on the rocks. "Mind you, it has nothing to do with the fact that Miss Roseline and I were in actual danger today, danger for our lives. We're only citizens like the rest of Americans. It's a matter of policy."

"Policy you were utterly opposed to only four hours ago," Jessup said coldly.

"Has nothing to do with it," the senator repeated as he held his glass out for a refill. "Nothing at all. It's the American way."

Nile Barrabas turned his back in disgust and looked out the window of the suite once more. It was the way American policy was decided, he knew, but seeing it in action didn't make it any easier to stomach. Let the old man sell America's edge down the river. The SOBs would be there for him.

"Why are we here?" Nile suddenly said out loud, startling the whole group in the suite but not turning around to face them.

"What do you mean?" the senator asked, unsure what was going on.

"You wanted us here to talk to you. You had Jessup bring me and Beck to Hartford for some reason. What was it?"

"He thought better of it," Miss Roseline said from her perch. "It was nothing."

No one could see Nile's sarcastic expression. He knew that the senator's original purpose for wanting them at the fair had been the same as Jessup's: to check out the exhibits and see what was on sale that might be dangerous for the U.S. But the near-accident had put things in a real personal perspective for the senator. Now he was mollified and wanted the SOBs to go away. It was a change in plans. There was no true need to keep anyone from prying into America's secrets, and the wheels of commerce needed to be lubricated. The "muscle" of America wasn't a top priority anymore.

Barrabas faced the occupants of the room with a still but dangerous look on his face, then spoke calmly. "We're leaving then, gentlemen, Miss Roseline. See you later." He turned to Jessup. "Walker, make sure you bill the senator for our time, for this consultation, will you? Wouldn't want to think this has been a waste of a day. Come on Beck, we can get a commuter hop down to New York."

"I'm going home to New London, if it's okay with you, boss," Beck said in a depressed voice. "They have commuter jobs down there from Bradley, as well."

"Whatever you want. There's nothing for us here."

No one stopped the fighting men from leaving the Hilton. They slammed the door behind themselves and walked to the elevator and pushed the button for the lobby. It hadn't been their show, after all.

4

Nikoli Geogi was shown into the executive offices of Continental Air Systems Ltd. on the penthouse floor of the Continental Building in New York.

"Mr. Geogi! How good of you to come to visit us." The president and chairman of the board of Continental, his face flushed with pleasure, came around his desk to shake Nikoli's hand. The warm greeting was a small clue to just how much Jason Rabinowicz wanted a big sale for his company. He would have met with Geogi anywhere for the opportunity to give a pitch.

"Have a seat, please. Coffee? A cocktail?" Rabinowicz asked fervently.

"Perhaps just a coffee, black, if you will." Nikoli smiled as Rabinowicz gave hurried orders to his secretary. The red-carpet treatment was a lot different from the kind of reception a man like Nikoli had gotten used to on his previous assignments. It was clearly more comfortable to be a captain of commerce than it was to run a spy network. The perks were incomparable in this life he had now.

Of course, the spymaster's little tricks hadn't hurt in making the transformation. He had been able to do some background work on Continental that had been much more extensive than even the most advanced industrial spy's could have been. Sources were available to him around the world that no private company could hope to duplicate.

Nikoli had found out that Continental had poured all its money into the development of the Panther air traffic system. The transformation of the system from its origins as the foundation of the United States' air defense had been much more complex than anyone had assumed, and until recently the U.S. government's insistence on keeping the derivative traffic control system top-secret had crushed Continental's hopes for quickly recouping its investment.

"It's so fortunate for you that the Senate has reversed itself concerning the availability of the Panther to foreign markets," Nikoli said as he sipped the hot coffee Rabinowicz's secretary had just put before him.

"Well, yes!" Rabinowicz said as he took his seat behind the huge mahogany desk again. "We're delighted, of course."

"Though you will have quite a time getting the orders quickly enough, won't you?"

Rabinowicz looked at Geogi suspiciously. He was sitting down with the devil, and he knew it, but he still thought he could determine some of the cards that would be dealt in this game. Geogi's words hinted that he knew much more about the shaky financial condition of the huge aerospace firm than Rabinowicz would ever want anyone to know. Especially anyone he was going to be facing over a bargaining table. Especially anyone as dangerous as this man.

"We are convinced that we'll pull in more than enough orders to make this an extremely good year for Continental," Rabinowicz said stonily.

Geogi drank the last of the coffee and put the cup on the desk. "A good year for profits, as well? Or just a good year for lobbying and public relations? After all, you've been sitting on the costs of research and development for quite some time. Certainly you need to have a great deal of cash flow quite soon to cover that. I don't question the undoubtable value of what's been happening in Washington. I just wonder if the Pentagon has strung you along for so many years that it is questionable whether you are going to survive."

"Of course we'll survive!" Rabinowicz rose indignantly from his seat, acting as though his mother's virtue had just been attacked.

"Now, now, Mr. Rabinowicz, let's not play games. You needn't worry, I don't intend to use your predicament to cause you or your company any harm."

"Actually, Mr. Geogi, as much as I'm interested in hearing you out, I don't think there's any business we can do." Rabinowicz suddenly acquired a righteous expression. "You must know that various people in the United States Senate have put pressure on our military to release some aspects of the Panther system from restricted use so that we can begin the long work of installing our technology in civilian airports. The Pentagon was able to add to that legislation very considerable restrictions on our international trade. There's no way I could ever allow the sale of our Panther system to the Soviet Union. Never."

"Not even for one hundred million dollars for a single system?"

Rabinowicz was stunned into silence.

Geogi looked at him steadily. "Could I have some more coffee, please, Mr. Rabinowicz? Then perhaps you and I can talk."

JASON RABINOWICZ SAW IT ALL before him: he could save his company—more than that, he could make it rich—with a single deal. The deal was with the sworn enemy of the United States. There was little doubt that this enemy would take apart a civilian Panther system and come up with major new advances in its own air defense system rather than use it for purely commercial purposes. There was no question that the Russians must want the system for purposes other than civilian.

Rabinowicz's mind had been working overtime in the hour since Nikoli Geogi had appeared in his office. He had a whole line of rationalizations in place to justify the deal. For one thing, the man was an official of the "new" Soviet Union. *Glasnost* and the recent statements of General Secretary Gorbachev were changing America's image of Russia, which meant it was improving on the image of the "evil empire."

Rabinowicz was also allowing himself to be convinced of the excuses—the covers, really—that Nikoli Geogi had put forth. The Panther system wasn't actually meant for the Soviet Union. It was for Colombia, a South American country that was hardly on the excluded list of U.S. trading partners. Even if Rabinowicz's suspicion that some official of the notoriously corrupt Colombian regime had provided the Soviets with an easily purchased fake set of docu-

ments was true, was it his job to do the investigative
work of the State Department?

There were dozens of possible excuses that Rabinowicz could make to color this deal so he wouldn't feel
guilty. Maybe the Soviets were beginning to send foreign aid to Colombia, he thought, and maybe they had
defined the Colombian civilian air traffic problem as
a major issue for that country, one that would justify
the investment of so much money. Because, in fact,
the hundred million dollars that Geogi was talking
about was a very high price for the Panther, one that
Continental had never hoped to receive for one of the
systems.

All of that was working in Rabinowicz's brain, but
there was a cloud over it, one that he couldn't wipe
away.

"How do you dare to do this?" he finally broke
down and asked Geogi. "Why do you think you can
take the risk of walking in and offering this deal?
What makes you think that I won't call Washington
the minute you leave? You didn't even bother with a
good cover—if you had, you'd have sent some paid
Colombian stooge in here rather than come yourself,
when it's known you're attached to the Soviet mission to the United Nations."

Geogi leaned back in his chair and casually folded
his arms behind his head. He was a handsome man,
and his stylish London suit didn't conceal the fact that
he had a well-maintained body. His smiling eyes
showed how quick his brain was. "Any good businessman knows one must learn about the people he's
dealing with, dear Mr. Rabinowicz. There are always
such interesting things to discover that might be use-

ful. There is, for instance, your mother-in-law, a lovely lady. Still in Riga, isn't she? I understand your wife adores her.''

Rabinowicz collapsed back against his chair with so much force that it appeared he'd been struck physically. "You wouldn't."

"Of course I would. Without the slightest hesitation. Your wife was able to leave Latvia during the war. I understand that she grew up in Great Britain, thinking that she'd been one of the multitude of Jewish orphans who'd been taken in by the English after they'd been smuggled out of the territory occupied by the Nazis. It must have come as a shock to her when it was discovered that her mother survived because she'd been hidden by her townspeople and hadn't been taken to any of the death camps, as had been assumed.

"There were many tearful reunions, as I remember. And there are many letters and phone calls to this day. Many of them have to do with the old woman's desire to emigrate to Israel. A shame, a woman like that, who has endured so much, to be denied her final wish."

"You mean..."

"The list of people who are allowed to emigrate is very small, and their number is increasingly taken up by the political, literary and artistic dissidents your leaders enjoy promoting to the status of media stars," Geogi said sourly. "There is little chance a simple retired factory worker from Riga could make the list. However, certain people in Moscow who I know would be willing to consider special circumstances..."

"You're asking me to give you one of the most valuable pieces of American technology in return for the freedom of my mother-in-law? You're offering me the one thing that would make my wife happy in return for my treason."

"Especially since your wife has so little time in which to be happy."

Rabinowicz couldn't even react to the brutality of that statement. "How could you possibly have found out—she doesn't even know herself. The doctors—"

"A tragedy, a woman in the prime like that, struck down by a strange and untreatable cancer. What do they suspect? Six months? A year, if luck is on your side?"

"You are a monster," the industrialist said, but he knew the insult was without meaning. He knew that he was defeated. The simple economics of the deal and the idea of saving the company his father and he had built up from nothing had taken him right up to the line. But to give Reba this last present, to let her see the fulfillment of her mother's dream before she herself died, was something that was impossible for him to pass up.

He knew that he was indeed doing business with the devil, and he was prepared to sell his soul.

"Talk specifics, then, Geogi. Forget the games. You know I'm in. You know I'll deliver under these conditions. What's the price? What's the delivery schedule? How are you going to pull this off?"

Nikoli Geogi smiled pleasantly. "I told you we could do business together, Mr. Rabinowicz. A simple trade, something I need for something you want. It's the capitalist system at work, isn't it?"

ONE MONTH LATER, two ships were at a dock on the Brooklyn waterfront, end to end. The first was the *Don Quixote*, a freighter under Colombian registry. The other was the *Constantine*, a Romanian craft of similar size.

To any inquiring eyes, they were simply two unrelated cargo ships that happened to be sharing a pier. Even the FBI, which routinely monitors Soviet-bloc shipping in American ports, hadn't discovered any connection between them. The *Don Quixote*'s papers were perfectly in order. It was in Brooklyn to deliver a shipment of coffee and to load technical products, the most lucrative of American exports.

The *Constantine* was in Brooklyn to take on a load of American grain products. It had been another bad year for Eastern bloc agriculture, and the pressures of Romanian domestic consumption had forced Moscow to bend its rules once more and admit its dependence on the United States for food by allowing its satellites to spend their limited amounts of hard currency for the American agricultural surplus.

It appeared to be only coincidental that the grain and the technological products were both stored in the same warehouse, which belonged to the Long Island Chandlery Company. Only a much more thorough investigation would have disclosed that the company had only recently been purchased by the import-export corporation of the Romanian People's Republic. Even then, with the recent rush of international trade between the United States and Romania, only the most suspicious eyebrows would have been raised.

Agent Timothy Marchand was going through the motions with an understated air of boredom. "It's my duty to go over your end use permit, Captain Ruloz."

The end use permit was a guarantee that the restricted materials wouldn't be reexported from the country to which they were being sent. When the most important American technological devices were involved, it was imperative that there be some restrictions on what happened to the items when they left immediate American control.

Captain Ruloz, used to the routine, handed over the sheaf of papers and went back to his own paperwork. "There's everything you need, Marchand. You know me. Clean as a whistle. Bring in no dope, take out no contraband."

"Yeah, yeah." Marchand waved away the protest with a cynical look. "You're the only Colombian who's not involved in cocaine and marijuana. What, was your father a priest or something? That what made you so pure?"

"Marchand!" Ruloz looked up, shocked. "A priest, he can't have children. They take the vow, celibacy, you know? No way. I'm a good man. I have honor."

"Honor, in Colombia?" The tough agent had seen it all in his years working for the Customs Department. "Everything and everyone's got his price, Ruloz. Everyone."

"Not me, and not Continental, for Christ's sake! Marchand, you're dealing with the cleanest Colombian shipping firm. It is transporting the goods and products of one of the Fortune 500. You are crazy if you think any of us are going to get involved in illegal stuff."

"Shove it, Ruloz." Marchand put the papers back down on the captain's desk and stood up. "You're in order. I'll clear you with the harbor pilot. You're off in another hour, right?"

"On schedule, as always."

"Spare me the commercial. You're clean. Let me out of here. I have to go check the Commies tied up here."

"The life of intrigue you live!" Ruloz said with a sneer. Obviously his feelings had been hurt by Marchand's attitude, and that was his way of getting back.

"I know, clean Colombians and honest Romanians. That's exotic for you! I love it when stereotypes are broken." Sarcasm dripped from Marchand's voice. "It makes you realize the common humanity that still exists in this world of ours."

Marchand left and walked onto the pier. He moved up to the Romanian ship and went through the same procedure.

Later that night, the *Don Quixote* and the *Constantine* both sailed out of New York harbor, just two more moderate-size ships in the flotilla of craft moving the lifeblood of international trade through the port.

"You still here, Marchand?" Tom Delany, one of the paper-shufflers at the customs department asked when he found the agent standing in the window overlooking the Narrows, the gateway to New York harbor.

"Yeah, Tom. Just one of those nights I'm not going to get home as early as I'd like. Just one of those nights to think."

"What's bugging you?" Delany asked. He wasn't used to Marchand or any of the other customs agents going through a great deal of anxiety over their jobs. They were like air traffic controllers upon whose work hundreds of lives depended every day.

"Something about that Romanian ship..."

"Hey, you guys went the extra mile on that. You went into the hold, you checked the crates, and there was nothing but food in there."

"Yeah." Marchand sighed and turned around. He pulled his coat off the rack by the door and put it on. "I'll forget it. The damned paperwork that goes into international trade—especially with the Commies— you just get spooked, I guess, thinking there might be something very important that gets past you. The hours in this job, they're getting to me, that's what it must be. I haven't seen my kids awake in so long I forget whether my oldest son shaves yet. I need a vacation."

"Well, forget the Romanians and all the rest of it. Sending stuff to make bread to some satellite isn't enough to get you all wound up, Marchand. It just isn't. Take that vacation, you deserve it."

Marchand forced a smile. "Will do, soon. Tell Uncle Sam you agree, will you? Maybe he can ease up on some of this forced overtime and give me a break."

"And, Marchand, if your son does shave now, make sure you get him a real razor. None of those electronic things for wimps. That's what makes all those brokers such yuppies—they never learned to shave like men. I'm convinced of it!''

"I wish to God it was that easy, Delany. All I can say is, you make a statement like that and it's clear you never raised a boy of your own. Teaching some kid to be a man is the hardest thing in the world. Everything's against them, against them being real men. Hell, I've forgotten what a real man is myself."

TIMOTHY MARCHAND SAT on the nearly empty subway car as it hurtled its way through the tunnels under the East River, traveling from Brooklyn into Manhattan.

The noise of the modern train seemed so soothing, so calm, compared to the old ones. Marchand knew they were produced in West Germany, and it was just one more example of American dependency on foreign goods.

We can't even make our own subways anymore, he thought to himself.

The train was almost empty, as it was well past midnight on a weekday. On Saturday there probably would have been many more people traveling to Manhattan for a night on the town. But Tuesdays just didn't produce that kind of energy in folks. It was a workday, and only people like Marchand who had to put in late hours were caught out at that time of night.

He looked around and studied the few people who were in the car with him. An elegantly dressed man was sitting alone, midway up the car. Marchand decided to make up a story about the guy. Why would anyone dressed that well be in a New York subway on a Tuesday night?

It was easy to come up with a whole episode in the gentleman's history. He had a secret Italian mistress in Brooklyn, a woman-of-the-earth type he went to see when his frigid wife wouldn't know, at strange hours of the night or day. It had been one of those times when the man simply had to see his woman and he'd taken a risk he shouldn't have by going to Brooklyn. They'd had their night of passion and their hours of regret about their circumstances, and now the man, sad and tired, was headed back to his reality.

The rest of the people defied Marchand's weak excursion into fiction. Two bums, not taking much notice of each other, were probably part of the omnipresent homeless. There might be something tragic about them, but their dirty bodies and their foul smell of stale alcohol made it difficult for Tim to grant them a place in literature. Leave that for the real writers out there, who could find a novel in thin air.

He didn't want to fictionalize anything about the other people in the subway. A young black couple were at the very end of the car, making out softly and gently. There was an eroticism to them, just the way they were so carefully expressing their affection with gentle touches. Their reality was so pleasant that he didn't want to mess with it and create anything else.

He smiled to himself as he thought of his son doing just that someday. Hell, maybe the kid was already doing it! How would Marchand know? He hadn't spent any time with the kid in so long that his remarks to Delany hadn't been bull. Tim loved his son. What were the dreams he'd had? That the two of them would go to the Mets games together, and the Knicks and the Islanders. That they'd fish in the Catskills, maybe get a boat and do some deep-water angling out on Long Island Sound.

That kind of sharing was important and meaningful, much more so than the yelling about haircuts and the constant pressure to make the kid do better in school. It was times like this, when he missed his son very much, that Marchand really regretted that only those base parental functions had been part of their recent time together.

He should take a vacation, no matter how undermanned the office was. It had been true! He didn't know for sure if the kid was shaving yet! These were the best years for a father and his son, and they were years that would never come back again if they were missed.

The subway approached Marchand's stop. The well-dressed guy stood up when Tim did. The train came to a halt and the doors slid open. The station was deserted except for the old lady in the change booth, quietly listening to her radio and undoubtedly hoping that there would be no business for a long while so she could enjoy her well-paid solitude.

Marchand went back to his story-making and walked up the stairs to Lexington Avenue. He'd turn at the street and go toward the middle-class Yorktown area. It was one of the very few parts of Upper Manhattan where a regular family could still afford the rent and the services of life in the city. The gentleman was from someplace much more expensive and pricey than that. He'd probably head for the river, toward the high-rent skyscrapers that lined the water and cost more per square foot than Marchand could pay for his entire three-bedroom apartment.

The sounds of the street took over after Tim had ascended to Lexington, and he forgot all about the fiction he'd been creating.

His stomach was taking control. Maybe the little woman had stayed up—she did sometimes, just to be there when he got home. When that mood struck her, it always meant a special treat for him. She'd be in her most domestic spirit and would insist on making a full meal for him. If not, it was another sandwich or some leftovers to pop into the microwave and eat alone, watching the wasteland of late-night television.

Tim turned off Lexington and walked up the street. The city had been cutting back, and the first areas to see the frugality were always the residential neighborhoods where the high and mighty didn't live. Bulbs were missing in some of the street lamps, and two abandoned cars squatted by the curb, their wheels and other parts stripped for weeks.

Marchand just walked past them and didn't pay attention. This was his home. That was all.

"Mr. Marchand!" Somebody had called out his name, and it wasn't any great surprise. At other places in New York a guy might be totally anonymous, but not in an area like Yorktown, where he'd grown up, been married and sired a family.

Tim turned around and realized that the person who had called his name was the well-dressed gent from the subway. That was a surprise. Tim was sure they hadn't met before.

"Mr. Marchand, I'm sorry to bother you," the man said as he walked up to him. "It seems that we have a problem, you and I."

"Problem?" Tim asked. All he needed was for the guy to turn out to be one of the loony-tunes of Manhattan. Don't judge a book by its cover or a man by his clothes anymore. "Look, Mac, I got no problem with you. The biggest problem I got is trying to find some time to take my son fishing."

"I think I can solve that one for you," the man said. His speech betrayed a hint of an accent. The English was excellent—there was no doubt about that—but something in the inflection of the correct words made Tim Marchand think of some place other than New York. It made him even warier than he had been before.

"Don't try and solve anything for me, mister. I'm going home."

Marchand began to walk away. There was a strange sound behind him, like something rubbing against cloth. It was just strange enough that Tim fought his better instincts to keep on going and turned to see what had caused the sound.

The man was still standing there, handsome and debonair in his trench coat and three-piece suit. He looked just as sophisticated as he had before, with the exception of a deadly-looking knife in his hand that went a long way to transform his image.

"Shit," Tim said, much too softly.

The man lunged at him. The blade was held outward in his hand, and the sharp steel caught a ray of the light from one of the lamps that was still working. An errant glint reflected suddenly and bizarrely in Tim's eyes.

Marchand lifted both his forearms without thinking to ward off the slash, which was aimed right at his throat. The blade sank into the flesh in his forearm and sliced downward, tearing through his overcoat and shirt.

The wetness was the only thing Tim registered. The pain hadn't come yet. There was only the river of his blood. He wanted to cover the wound and stanch the flow, but a more primal need to continue to protect his neck was in control of his actions.

Thoughts ran through his mind crazily. There was no hope of fighting this guy. He was a pro—Tim could tell by the way he was holding the knife. It rose into the air again and once more caught a glint of light from a distant street lamp.

The knife slashed through the air, followed by the sudden sound of air escaping from Tim's left lung. The blade had cut between two of his ribs and punctured his chest.

Help! There had to be help somewhere. He finally opened his mouth to scream, forgetting all the images of manhood that had made him want to do this one-on-one at first. The time wasn't right for heroics, and heroics weren't going to suddenly give him the skills to fight someone who was better trained than he was.

But the knife was being pulled out of his lung now, accompanied by a sharp, horrible pain in his side. Tim lowered his hands from their position as guardians of his neck and grasped the burning area of his body. There wasn't strength to scream now, there was only the damned pain.

And the horrible, terrible regret that he never would go fishing with his son.

Then, when Tim wasn't even looking, the knife found its original target. The slash opened up the jugular vein in his neck, and the flow of blood down over Tim's body was much more copious than it had been before.

He didn't notice, because there was no blood getting to his brain to keep his senses alive and alert. It was all pouring out of him and onto the sidewalk, forming an instant scarlet river.

As he folded up, Tim's knees hit the asphalt hard enough for him to register one more jolt of pain. Then it was over. He didn't feel the impact of his head crashing onto the pavement.

Nikoli Geogi stepped back and looked around, checking once more to make sure there were no witnesses on the deserted late-night street. He checked his clothing to make sure he'd avoided its being stained by any of the gushing blood the knife wounds had caused.

Then he turned and moved quickly back toward Lexington Avenue. Sure that his gloves had covered fingerprints, he threw the knife into a garbage can and smiled at the sense of accomplishment he had. The tension of not being in the field had been getting to him lately.

The news that there had been a suspicious customs agent at the pier that night had been enough to justify his going into action. Time wasn't at their disposal to call in any of the regular operatives, and he couldn't take the chance that the man had discovered anything or had even harbored a suspicion about the cargo switch that had taken place between the two ships.

The Panther was on its way to Riga now. It was imperative that it reach its destination without incident. It was little things like too-inquisitive customs agents that fouled up such a complex piece of industrial espionage and illegal exportation.

However much warmth there might be in the joint statements made at all the recent summits attended by the superpowers, it was still men like Geogi who were going to be the backbone of the Soviet's position in the world—men who were willing to act when action was necessary.

When he got to the bright lights of the avenue, Nikoli made one more searching sweep of the neighborhood to make sure there wasn't anyone following him or trying to identify him. A tall man in a trench coat who had never really been in the direct rays of any of the few working street lamps wasn't a description that any New York police would be able to use. A dead body on the pavement in Manhattan wasn't anything special enough to raise suspicion itself. Murder was too much a way of urban life in America.

Geogi, of course, had an ironclad alibi, if he ever needed it. Besides, he also enjoyed diplomatic immunity if he ever needed to resort to it.

All in all, a simple operation. Nikoli lifted up his hand to wave down a cab barreling up Lexington. One thing he needed no more of was an American subway.

He smiled as he gave the driver the destination and sat back in the rear seat in contentment. Things were going well, and he could take a special satisfaction in a job well done.

There really should be more action like this in his life, he thought. It made things so very much more real than parties at the United Nations.

5

Julijis Stucka stood at the back of the hall and watched while Janis Valters performed for the screaming audience that packed the auditorium. The sight disgusted him.

Janis's hair had been styled—though Julijis would never have used that word to describe it—with thick mousse that molded strands of it into sharp spikes. Janis wore dancing tights of a matching purple color, with fabric so elastic it clung to every contour of his muscular legs. Janis's torn shirt was simply another way of flaunting convention and respectability.

Janis's contortions while he sang into the microphone only intensified Julijis's revulsion and added to his opinion that the performance was loud and vulgar. Julijis quickly went through the list of offenses for which the younger man could have been arrested only a couple of years earlier.

This was the result of *glasnost*, Julijis thought with contempt. Rock stars in X-rated clothing, yelling fans adoring a cult of media personality, it all illustrated a fatal weakening of the moral fabric of the Soviet Union.

Janis sang a Latvian translation of the lyrics of Bruce Springsteen's "My Hometown," a melancholy ballad about the changes that were going on in a small village unable to fight the ravages of time and a national economy that paid no attention to human values. If it had been presented as a critique of American society Julijis would have applauded the performance, but it was clear to him and the audience that the words were directed not at Washington but at Moscow. The musician was using the performance as a platform to make political points he would never have dared make in a public speech, even in light of the new openness. Julijis knew that the words to the song meant one thing to Janis, that they were a populist creed to the young rebel, but to Julijis they were words of disintegration of the Party's place in the world.

My hometown, indeed! Julijis thought with a sneer of contempt as he turned and left the auditorium. He spoke to one of the guards from his detachment, which was posted in the lobby of the building. "You, don't let this get any further out of hand than it already is."

The militiaman, anxious to impress a superior, blushed furiously. "Sir!" he answered smartly. He knew Stucka was a hard man to please and that he was well known in the barracks as the most severe disciplinarian in the entire Latvian militia.

Julijis was glad to leave the building then. He was after something much bigger than overseeing rock concerts these days. When he was on the streets of Riga, he moved quickly in the direction of the Naval Institute on the waterfront. That was where the bigger pickings were.

The new assignment was a godsend. If he made sure the job was done well, there was surely a promotion in it for him, and a promotion might finally get him out of Riga.

While the civilians of the city believed they were the most fortunate of all Soviet citizens, Julijis thought he was in a trap. The biggest block for a Soviet bureaucrat in his career advancement was to be labeled as a member of an ethnic minority. No matter what the public pronouncements of the government and the party leaders, the truth was that ethnic Russians ruled the Soviet Union. It was all well and good to think of the Party transcending linguistic and racial differences, but it was a pretense, and everyone understood that.

The modern Soviet Union was as much a Russian Empire as anything under the Tsars. It was convenient for the leaders in Moscow to have functionaries like Julijis who would gladly oversee their own countrymen, but it was quite something else for them to see a Latvian militiaman as someone who might dictate or translate Party policy for Russians.

The barriers to advancement that a Latvian or a Tartar or an Armenian faced might be publicly denounced as often as Americans denounced racism in their country, but the reality was just as concrete. It was only the very exceptional Latvian who was ever trusted by Moscow, and Julijis knew that.

He also knew it was unfair. His father had, after all, been the most fervent supporter of every Moscow regime from the beginning. The older Stucka had gladly turned in any countrymen who had been suspected of lack of loyalty to the Party. When the Soviet armies had entered Latvia near the end of the Second World War, Stucka had been happy to go around the neighborhoods of Riga with the KGB officials who were looking for anyone who had collaborated with the Germans during the occupation.

That his best friends and co-workers were among the multitude who had been sent to the Gulag had never fazed Stucka. Looking back on that dark chapter of history, Julijis never even thought of questioning or criticizing his father. The man had done his job for the Party and the State, and his willingness to put aside personal affiliations for the larger good was one of his most admirable qualities.

Both generations of Stuckas had been willing to go along with the vagaries of policy that came out of Moscow. If there were to be changes, it was the duty of loyal soldiers not to question them but to see them through. The purges mandated by Stalin, the militarization imposed by Khrushchev, and everything else in between had been accepted on faith by the Stuckas. Even now, as difficult as the seeming reversal was, Julijis could follow the new orders from Moscow, within reason.

He was one of the many who was convinced that there would be a reassessment of the current situation. The iron hand of the state was necessary to continue the progress the Soviet Union had been making in its military race against America. One by one, regimes all over the world were coming into the Communist sphere. Julijis and his fellow ideologues were convinced that the war in Afghanistan would be won, and Nicaragua would become a seedbed of progressive Communist policy in Central America. Ethiopia's government would maintain its march on the tribes of its country and turn it into a socialist state.

With such a string of successes there could be no doubt that true hard-line Party members would direct the Soviet Union correctly, eliminating deviance such as Janis's rock band, when the time came to remove the liberals from their positions of power in the Kremlin.

All in time. That was all that was required, a little more waiting. Julijis was pleased by the thought. His salute to the guards outside the Naval Institute was smart and accompanied a very uncharacteristic smile on his face.

He marched past the sentries and into the old building. It had been constructed in the ornate fashion that Stalin had admired, with hints of Greek architecture in the huge columns and in the enormous open space of its lobby, a style providing inspiring vistas and encouraging elevated thought.

The Naval Institute was the center of research and development for the Soviet war machine. Just then, it was a beehive of very practical activity. Big things were happening, and Julijis was in charge of their care.

"General!" Julijis snapped to attention when he greeted Nikoli Geogi in the inner sanctum of the institute. Geogi looked at the overanxious Latvian and laconically returned the greeting.

"Captain Stucka, I had expected you earlier."

The Latvian swallowed with difficulty. Geogi was exactly the type of commander Julijis wanted to become. General Geogi's exploits in the espionage field were legend throughout the Soviet military. Julijis kicked himself for having been distracted by his personal anger with Janis Valters and spending so much time at the rock concert. He wanted nothing more than to make points with the general. He would have to strive harder to make himself even more of a model soldier in Geogi's eyes. If he could prove himself to this man, then he could pass muster in front of any Russian general and perhaps get himself out of Latvia.

"The team from Moscow will be here tomorrow to greet the ship. The *Constantine* should arrive in two days, exactly on schedule, according to our most recent reports. I expect the Naval Institute to be on top alert. There must, however, be nothing to draw undue attention to any ongoing activity. One of the reasons we chose the port of Riga was our expectation that most Western intelligence concentrates on Leningrad and Odessa these days. Also, if we're correct, there is no real suspicion about the work we'll be doing in Riga. There shouldn't be any reason for anyone to suspect that the Panther computer system is here.

"Assign your men accordingly. Keep as many inside as you can. Try to arrange a security system that will not have uniformed militiamen conspicuously in the public view."

"Yes, sir!" Julijis saluted again.

Geogi went back to the plans that were spread out on his desk and began to study them again. "Get to work, Captain. I want a thorough presentation of your scheme within twenty-four hours."

"Yes, sir!" Julijis repeated, then spun around and marched out of the office and straight out of the building. He headed back to his own office in the militia headquarters building. He'd stay up all night if necessary to fulfill Geogi's command. There would be no holes in the security for the Naval Institute, not while there was anything of such importance going on near Julijis, something of such great importance that its proper execution could mean his promotion out of Latvia.

THE FINAL CHORUS SOUNDED. It was accompanied by loud, reverberating chords on the electric guitars. The crowd went crazy with adulation and applause.

"Janis! Janis!" they screamed as he took his last bow and ran off the stage. His costume was soaked with sweat. Once he was behind the curtain, he rubbed his forearm across his face to wipe away the drenching perspiration.

Koren ran up to him and ignored the wetness. She threw her arms around him for a tight embrace. "It was a wonderful performance tonight." She bent her head onto Janis's chest and rubbed her hair against his bare skin.

"Great job, Janis!" Andrievs had come up and was slapping Janis on the back. "Man, we really gave them music tonight!"

Janis gently put Koren aside and reached for a towel one of the stagehands was holding out for him. He used it to sop up the sweat. He looked from his girlfriend to his best friend in the band. "But did they hear our words?" Janis asked quietly. "It means nothing to just put out sounds if they're not paying attention to what we're saying."

It was as though Janis had brought an end to a New Year's Eve celebration. Both Andrievs and Koren moved away from him, and their smiles disappeared.

"You are making too much trouble in that way, Janis," Koren said. "You must remember that we are always watched."

"If only we were watched as closely by our fans for an interpretation of the words we sing as we are by the militia," Janis grumbled.

The other two said nothing, and Janis forced himself to be more upbeat. "I have to take a shower, then we'll go to Knighthood Square for a drink, okay? Something to toast tonight."

Koren and Andrievs were made more cheerful by the offer and attempted to permanently shrug off their negative spirits. They struggled to be in a party mood. "Fine," Koren said through a forced smile. "We can all use a celebration."

THE NIGHT WAS WARM ENOUGH for them to enjoy the outdoor tables without coats or jackets. They were sipping vodka, the mainstay of the Latvian people just as it was of the Russian overlords.

"There was a man from *Pravda* there at the concert," Koren was saying. With Janis showered and dressed and seemingly in a good mood, she'd regained much of her animation. "Do you think there will be a review?"

"Probably not," Andrievs said soberly. He was always the most pragmatic of the group. "*Pravda* seldom reviews the arts, of any kind, and certainly not rock music. If they write anything, it will be a social commentary on the impact of decadent Western music on Latvia and will use it as a reason to call for stronger controls on what goes on in the Baltic states. *Pravda* still thinks we're too close to Sweden and Finland and that our morals are being corrupted by their television."

Koren gave Andrievs an exasperated look. "It's hard enough to keep Janis's mind straight about all this political bull. You don't have to make it any harder."

"Don't worry," Janis said soothingly. "I'm not worried about what the political press will say about us. The Riga newspapers love us—they have all along—and their reviewers were at the concert in force."

"The provincial newspapers can't make you a star!" Koren protested. "They can only make you a bigger fish in a much-too-small pond. We need attention from Moscow."

"Koren," Janis said calmly, "if that comes, it will happen. I know that good musicians can have wonderful careers—look at Springsteen. I'm not going to run away from fame. It brings me a larger audience to listen to my message. But I'm also not going to turn my back on Latvia. This is our homeland. Our songs are in Latvian, not Russian. Our souls are Latvian, not Russian. If we try too hard to make it otherwise, we will—"

"Mr. Valters." Janis stopped when he heard somebody call his name. The rock star looked around and realized that the voice had come from a man in his mid-thirties who looked uncomfortable amid the tables in Knighthood Square. He was holding his hat in hands that were rough and callused from hard work. His appearance was more like that of a peasant during the tsarist years than of the self-aware workers glorified by the Soviets.

Janis jumped up from his chair and moved to shake the other man's hand. "Peteris, what a surprise! Were you at the concert?"

"No, no, I don't go to such things. But I needed to talk to you, and they said you'd be here, so I came. I hope I'm not intruding...."

"Of course not!" Janis said, though both Andrievs and Koren had expressions on their faces that made the sentiment seem something short of universal. "Do you want a seat? Have a vodka with us!"

"No, thank you. But I have to talk to you." Peteris Danisevskis's tone and body language made it clear he wanted to talk to Janis alone.

"Of course," Janis said, his own voice changing to meet Peteris's serious intent. "Um, Koren, I'm afraid I'll have to go on home now. I'm sorry to leave you in the middle of a date...."

"It's been done before—and often," Koren said coldly.

Janis knew better than to let that conversation go on for any length of time. There was nothing to gain and everything to lose in continuing it and allowing Koren to drag him into territory that held nothing but anger and hostility on its charts. "Andrievs, good night. Great performance, man! The best, you're right. I'll see you at rehearsal tomorrow."

Janis followed Peteris away from Knighthood Square and toward the waterfront. Only when they'd gone a block from the café and were sure no one was following them did Janis dare speak to the man he knew to be one of the longshoremen of the port of Riga. "There must be something up if you dare to come and get me like that."

"There is, Janis. I can't figure it out, but something is going on at the docks. We decided that you had to be informed and come and see for yourself. If we didn't know the Soviet navy's plans, we'd swear it was some top-secret nuclear sub coming in. But our people in naval headquarters swear it's not anything like that. Our intelligence from them has always been accurate before.

"But something is definitely up. They're clearing out three piers. We doubt it's for three berthings: it must be that they want one so secure they don't want to have anyone that close to it. They've also announced some traffic detours for two nights from now. They're claiming that the streets need repair or cleaning or something foolish like that. Bogus, totally bogus. They just don't want anything along the route."

"Where does the path they're clearing lead to?" Janis asked.

"That's a strange one there," Peteris answered, obviously puzzled. "It goes right to the Naval Institute. What could they possibly be taking there? It's for scientists, that place. What could it be?"

"I don't know yet," Janis answered firmly, "but we're going to find out."

6

Walker Jessup surveyed his surroundings with a look that spoke of pleasure and anticipation. Ah, the glory of it! The wonder of being in New York. At least in that part of it. While the world read of the homeless being dragged off the sidewalks and being sent to psychiatric evaluation at Bellevue, while thousands lived in poverty in Harlem, while gang wars ate up the life of Chinatown, there was always the Upper East Side, a whole other world.

And in the center of it was Maxim's.

He had to stop for a moment from the very thought of it: dinner at Maxim's, the world's most famous restaurant. Food was an obsession to Jessup. His substantial girth was proof of the quantity of food he ate, but someone who saw only that evidence of the extent of his gluttony would miss a major element in his personality. Walker Jessup loved good food. It wasn't a belly made by beer. It wasn't a stomach fed by McDonald's.

The fat padding him was of the highest quality possible in the world. That was a midriff bulging with the riches of the finest kitchens in New York, in America, in the world!

And that night, on someone else's expense account, Walker Jessup was going to feed himself at the altar of Maxim's. He was experiencing an acute heightening of his senses and an almost carnal lust more powerful than any he ever directed at women. How could mere sex compare to what was in store for him?

He had gone to some trouble to perform his part in the preparation for tonight. Maxim's demanded formal wear of its clientele, the way a great cathedral demands its acolytes wear festive robes. His tuxedo seemed to have shrunk by several inches, and the tailor had been rude enough to suggest there wasn't enough fabric left to let it out sufficiently. In fact, three tailors had delivered the same opinion. A quick trip to Brooks Brothers had produced a new suit on short notice, and at very considerable cost, but nothing, Jessup knew, compared to the cost of the meal he was preparing to enjoy.

Price tags rung up in Walker's mind as quickly as the names of his favorite French wines. The meal would cost his host thousands. Oh, Jessup could just taste it now.

He continued to move through the streets again and soon found himself standing in front of the famed entrance. Maxim's had originated in Paris. It had only a few branches in the world, and the New York one was the newest. Jessup tried to force from his mind the fear that there might be glitches in the operation. Could it be that perhaps the roughest of rough spots hadn't been worked out yet?

Guilt as deep as he could imagine swept through Jessup's heart. How could he think of Maxim's in those terms? Better that he should sully the virtue of the President's wife than question the abilities of the world's best international kitchen.

With the renewed vigor of a new suitor, Jessup turned and walked through the entrance. There was more to life than just putting nutrition of one kind or the other through your esophagus. Food was one of the vital sources of pleasure for the human body. It deserved decoration and presentation, and it deserved the proper setting. Maxim's understood all that. As soon as the door had closed behind him, Jessup was encased in rococo extravagance. Every detail of the corridor leading to the dining room was done in the plushest red, the most demure pink or the most authoritative black.

The way was lined with liveried serving men, all of whom added to the sense of decorum with their gracious bows and not one single lingering stare at the bulk of Jessup's stomach. It was not the type of place where a man would ever be mocked for his consumption of the best; rather, overindulgence was a form of sainthood within those walls, and they all knew it.

Jessup carried his head higher with the thought. He wouldn't have to deal with any of those ridiculously hard-stomached mercenaries in a place like Maxim's. There would be no foolishness about low-calorie diets from tinny, tiny ladies sipping mineral water. This was a man's eating establishment. And proud of it!

"Monsieur," the maître d' said kindly in tones reserved for a kindred spirit when he saw Walker Jessup appear at the entrance to the dining room. "A reservation?" The question had been asked with the

softest voice, but Jessup knew it would have turned to hardest steel if the wrong answer had been given.

"Yes, I'm to meet Mr. Rabinowicz here."

"Of course, *monsieur*!" The name was obviously known and most likely was associated with memories of substantial tips. A French face that icy seldom melted so quickly and so thoroughly. "This way, please."

The officious maître d' turned and led Jessup down the few stairs onto the main floor. A few feet above that coveted area were the tables of Siberia, the crowded space in any restaurant to which the nobodies are consigned. It was there at the tables lining the formal dance floor that the real people ate, the ones Maxim's management wanted to be on display. Somebody who failed to recognize the prominent people proved his own ignorance of who was who in New York City. No one who understood "power dining" would make the mistake of admitting that he encountered strange faces. Ignorance is not bliss in the social climber's galaxy.

Jessup sighed with relief when he realized that they were heading for the end of the rows of tables. His host had had the common sense to understand that it would have been difficult for Jessup to slide into an ordinary seat and that the fashionably small chairs with their backs to the dance floor could have produced their own embarrassment. The end table of the row, however, gave a man with a manly build more space and kept his protruding bulk out of the line of traffic of waiters and waltzers alike.

"Jessup, I'm so glad you could come." Jason Rabinowicz stood up and offered a hand to Walker.

"Have a seat, please have a seat. I'm glad I was able to talk François into giving us this table. It means so much more privacy than the regular ones, with parties on either side."

"Yes, yes," Jessup said as he quickly picked up the menu and opened it to begin the experience by feasting his eyes on the delights. The caviar to begin, with the finest sour cream, the kind that would put the store-bought brands to utter shame! Soup? The lobster bisque sounded perfect, just what he wanted as a light intermission. A fish course, or was that too brazen? No! Anyone who suggested a meeting at Maxim's wasn't worried about expense or anything of the kind. Fish, of course! Imperial crab legs, the luscious white meat dripping with drawn butter and ready to melt in his mouth. For the main course? Oh, he should really and truly have one of the superbly sauced French dishes, but there was a rack of lamb here that was supposed to be simply perfect. He deserved it! After all, there was the cost of a new tuxedo to be considered.

"You know, this is very difficult for me, Jessup."

Walker looked up with utter sympathy. If anybody could understand how difficult it would be for anyone but a master of the art of gourmet to work his way through this menu of the gods, he could!

Rabinowicz, who had worn an apprehensive look, seemed to appreciate Walker's good spirits and calmed down a bit.

"After all, a man in my position isn't used to meeting someone like you in this way. Your contacts were probably right that this was the perfect place, somewhere no one would suspect us."

Preoccupied as he was, Jessup idly pondered the meaning of those words.

"But, damn it, I need your help!"

"Well, by all means. If not the caviar, begin with the pâté. It's beyond belief, so light you wonder how they've created it, and perfectly spiced."

Dumbfounded, Rabinowicz stared at Jessup. "Is this some trick? Are you wired with a recorder? Are you trying to lure me into something? I have enough problems already!" With that, Rabinowicz stood up and prepared to leave.

"Now, now, Mr. Rabinowicz," Jessup said in his sweetest tone of voice in an attempt to placate the man who was supposed to pick up the tab. "Let's not be rash. Please, take your seat. Let's have a cocktail and we'll talk."

Talk, after all, had been Rabinowicz's reason for the meeting. Jessup had forgotten himself in the midst of his reverie. There was an agenda to get through, and he'd have to endure the annoyance of it before he could move on to things of real importance, like food.

A waiter appeared magically and asked for their drink orders. Jessup had been dreaming of a Perrier-Jouët champagne, but Rabinowicz's outburst had dampened his spirits and made him think better of jumping right into the good stuff. A simple aperitif would have to do. Rabinowicz ordered a martini.

"Now, let's begin," Walker said as he put down the menu with all the regret of a Talmudic scholar turning away from the Scriptures.

"I'm told you have a lot of clout with certain members of the Senate, Mr. Jessup."

"Yes, in fact I know almost all of them. I'm not in the lobbying business, though—that's not my role."

"I know. You're 'the Fixer,' and have been since your days in the CIA. I was around then, in Vietnam, and I saw some of your work. You had quite a reputation."

"I worked for it."

Rabinowicz seemed to be staring at Jessup now, and his expression told the whole story: how could the Fixer have ended up looking like this? It was a topic that Jessup had no intention of discussing.

"Well, so long as you're aware that I do not lobby, tell me why you're interested in those connections."

Their drinks arrived. From the way Rabinowicz downed the first half of his martini, Jessup could see that there was certainly trouble here.

"There's a certain senator who's become very pushy about the Panther air traffic control system...."

"Of course, he had a recent personal problem with air safety and has turned it into a crusade of sorts."

"Yes, well, his assistant, a Miss Roseline, has been on our phones day and night demanding that a prototype be delivered to the FAA and that we go into immediate production upon approval of our design, which approval she is adamant we'll have almost immediately."

"Yes." Why wasn't the man jumping in the aisles? Jessup asked himself silently. The Senate appropriations for the Panther would make him a fabulously rich man. Instead of being so concerned, he should be overjoyed.

Rabinowicz took a deep breath. "There is no prototype."

"Of course there is. My men and I saw it at the trade show in Hartford. You can't tell me it was a fake because my technical advisers went over it with a fine-tooth comb. They were doing calibrations of its effectiveness right there on the spot with some of your people."

Rabinowicz bit his lower lip so hard he looked as though he might break the skin. He looked at Jessup with a beseeching expression in his eyes. "Is it really true you can fix anything?"

That kind of abject fear in another man meant only one thing to Jessup: his services were desperately needed. He should have ordered that champagne, after all. He was going to have whatever he wanted tonight, and for a lot of other nights in the future.

"I can fix a great number of things."

"Can you fix a case of treason?"

"That might be difficult to simply 'fix,'" Jessup said, wondering where the conversation was really leading.

There was no answer for a couple of beats. Rabinowicz swallowed the rest of his martini and then, with enough courage from the alcohol, stared Jessup full in the face. "I've sold out the United States. I'm a traitor. There is no prototype because the one we had is somewhere in the Soviet Union. I sold it to them. Now I have to get it back. I can pay for it. I can pay for anything you say is needed.

"There are more rumors about you, Jessup. My people in Washington say that a miracle seems to happen whenever you put your mind to it. It appears that you have some kind of fighting men at your disposal who appear when you need them and disappear when you don't need them. This federal contract is going to make me very wealthy, and it means my corporation is going to be one of the richest of the high-tech firms, and it will come overnight. But only if that prototype is recovered. Not just because it will cut production time for the senator's request in half if we have it in hand, but also because I can't live with the knowledge that I've sold out."

Rabinowicz suddenly became terribly somber, and there was a darkness about him. "And I sold out too late. My wife is dead. It doesn't matter anymore. She's gone. But I have children, and I don't want them to grow up thinking that their father is such a—"

"I think we should talk about this over something to eat," Walker said jovially. He could smell money, lots of money, which was always the case when personal guilt was combined with potential financial gain.

"The caviar, a double serving, with champagne," Walker said to the waiter who had suddenly appeared by their table. "He'll have the same."

When the waiter had gone, Jessup leaned forward, all business. "Now, Mr. Rabinowicz, just how did that Panther prototype get to the Soviet Union, and where the hell is it?"

"THE NEW DELI HAS a half-price special on corned beef," the senator said gleefully as Miss Roseline produced limp-looking white bread that contained grayish-colored pieces of something that was supposed to look like meat.

"Don't have any liquor here on Capitol Hill," the senator continued while he opened his sandwich. "The constituents wouldn't like it one bit. Just Diet Pepsi."

Jessup looked with utter disgust at the pile of stuff that had been put before him. He swept it away with the back of his hand. For once he was in charge of a meeting with the old man, and there was no need for him to desecrate his stomach and its still-rich memories of last night's dinner with that kind of slop.

"Senator, you have a very difficult problem. Luckily for you, I have a solution."

"Problem?" The senator looked up from his meal and stared at Jessup. "I'm not sure what you mean."

"Miss Roseline, I'm sure you could find a bottle of the senator's private stock of bourbon here someplace if you looked very hard," Jessup said, pressing his advantage. "I'm afraid I'll need some liquid to get through this difficult meeting, since my national pride and my concern for America's security is at stake."

"Don't give me that bull," the senator said. "What game do you have up your sleeve this time?"

"No game, Senator," Jessup replied, gloating, "just information that America's air defense has been breached and that your new pet program of air traffic safety is endangered."

"What!" Every once in a while, when he was truly provoked, the old man forgot himself and tried to rise up on his atrophied legs, propelled by anger and wrath. This was one of those times. Jessup would never know if it was the air defense issue that had gotten to him or the memory of his private jet nearly colliding with the 747 over Hartford. Whichever, Walker once again found himself in the driver's seat.

"The bourbon, Miss Roseline, if you please. Then we'll have a very cozy chat."

"THE SON OF A BITCH! How could he—"

"It was love, Senator, something I'm not at all sure you're familiar with."

The senator didn't rise to the bait on that one. He just continued to glower. "Love, indeed, and then his wife dies before it can happen, in any event."

"The man lost his senses. There's no reason to beat up on him now, and certainly no reason to bring him to trial. After all, it's a cut-and-dried insanity plea on his part—pressure, grief, all of that."

"Insanity! For a treasonous act!"

"Senator, the way the country's going, you can get off on an insanity plea for stealing Fort Knox with an army. Besides, we'll only undermine the nation's faith in corporate America more if we bring this out, and there is the fact that he's willing to pay the fee."

The senator's eyes narrowed. "The fee? For what?"

"For my team to go in and get the Panther back. The Russians couldn't have figured out the intricacies of the system in just a few days. My team could go in and get it, bring it out—"

"You don't even know where it is."

Jessup sipped the last of his bourbon and held it out for a refill. "Yes, I do."

"How did you find that out?" the senator demanded.

"Adonis."

That forced the old man back into his chair. "Adonis! But you can't take the chance of involving him and breaking his cover. He's been one of the most successful agents we've ever had in the Soviet Union." Then, after a moment's thought, he added, "How did he do this? Are you sure he's not a double agent? First he produces that material on the Soviet submarine fleet. Then he got the dope on the new bomber they're developing, now this?"

"Bourbon." That was all Jessup would say until the senator signaled to Miss Roseline to fill up the Fixer's glass. Even the senator had to admit he was intrigued by the situation.

"Adonis reports a mysterious unloading of a cargo in a ship at Riga. It's been taken to the Naval Institute there. The timing is right, and Adonis reports that the crew of the ship have whispered about a change of nationality and something funny with its papers. It's there, in Riga. What we need is a lightning-fast strike force to go in and at least destroy the prototype, hopefully to retrieve it."

"So Rabinowicz pays you to send in those people of yours, and you collect a huge fee and he goes free."

"Mr. Rabinowicz has paid enough in the past few days. We have no other choice but to go in anyhow, so why not let him pay the bill?"

"How much more than usual are you getting, Jessup? How many pieces of silver are you collecting?" The senator's voice dripped venom.

"I'm doing a service to my country—"

"Don't give me that. You and your team are becoming more and more difficult, moving farther and farther outside the perimeters of our national policy. This is just one more step in that direction...."

"No action, no Panther. No Panther, the country becomes naked to a Russian attack. And our air traffic system doesn't get its new technology."

"More near misses," Miss Roseline whispered in a voice that implied haunting memories for her.

And apparently for the senator, as well. "Damn you, make it work, make it work perfectly and quickly. You have two weeks, no more, not one day more. If the operation isn't successful, I'll have Rabinowicz's balls—and your head!"

The senator spun his wheelchair around and guided it forcefully out of the room.

"Make sure they do it right this time, Mr. Jessup," Miss Roseline said with a quavering voice. "America must have the Panther, and it must have it soon."

After she'd followed the old man out, Walker poured himself yet another glass of bourbon, sat back with his feet up on the mahogany desk and thought about how interesting life could sometimes be.

7

Maxwell White, the president of the All-Oklahoma Development Company, knew he had a surefire winner. The new interstate highway that cut across the Osage reservation had produced the perfect demographics for a new luxury motel for the ever-growing number of tourists descending on Oklahoma for a prepackaged, sanitized taste of the Old West.

"This will be one of the best things that ever happened to them," White said with pride as he looked over the Osage Arms. "They'll get jobs as busboys and dishwashers, and they'll get tips from the tourists for those fake rain dances." A motley-looking group of American Indians were lined up along the red ribbon that symbolically blocked the entrance to the Osage Arms, waiting for their first performance. They were all dressed in a kind of approach to the costume that other Americans thought they should wear: loincloths, moccasins, bone armor over their chests and long hair atop their painted faces.

It was all fake. The loincloths were worn over swimming trunks to make sure no one's sensibilities were offended. The moccasins came from a mail-order firm in Maine. The bone armor was plastic, manufactured in Japan. The long hair was fake, too.

There was Indian blood in the men's veins, but it wasn't pure Osage. And any Osage blood they did have in their bodies was obviously well diluted with alcohol.

The busloads of tourists were surrounding the "authentic" Indians and shooting at them with their disc cameras with as much firepower as Kit Carson and much better aim than George Custer. The bleary eyes of the hung-over troupe didn't register anything as the flashbulbs popped in their faces.

"Okay, Chief, time to start some dancing. The television crews from Tulsa are all set up, and the tourists are anxious to get inside for their lunches."

The head of the dancing company looked at Maxwell with complete boredom. He nodded once to the developer and then turned to his men. "Hit it."

One of the group held a small drum in his arms and began to thump out a simple series of beats. The rest of the men began to shuffle their feet to the repetitive sounds, intoning a series of groans as their chorus.

"The real thing!" Maxwell turned to one of the reporters from Tulsa and smiled. "This is just the thing to make sure that all the interstate traffic pulls off at the Osage Arms and spends a bucket of money on our local economy."

The television video cameras were going, recording the sad sight of the Indians and the wide-mouthed grin of the capitalist. Maxwell was in his glory. In just a few more minutes the very same cameras would record him and the mayor cutting the ribbon and officially opening the motel. The crowds of tourists he'd arranged to be present would flock inside and start spending a flood of money to generate his long-awaited profits.

Maxwell was smiling directly into the cameras, prepared to launch into the next stage of his speech, when the lenses suddenly veered away from him and back to the dancers.

"Jesus, look at that!" one of the reporters said. "Who is he?"

Maxwell spun around to search the area to see what could possibly have distracted attention from his own media extravaganza. He instantly saw what the problem was. There was someone there who had much more appeal than he did. Damn it, he thought savagely.

The man's skin was a deep red, the mark of a full-blooded Indian. He was well over six feet tall. His bare chest gleamed with a thin veneer of sweat that only accentuated his hard, chiseled muscles and brought out the sharp lines of his abdomen. His long hair, obviously not a wig, cascaded down over his shoulders. Although his face was handsome, he looked a little vacant, as though he might be on some mild kind of drug.

Just then, as though he'd waited for the moment when he'd have everyone's attention, the man grabbed the drum from the sole musician in the original group and began to bang out a much livelier rhythm. His feet started to keep pace with the new beat, and he began to sing in a guttural tone, one that had much more passion and meaning than what the other men had given the audience.

"Who the hell is that?" Maxwell demanded of Frank Hogan, his security chief. "Did you hire him?"

"Me? Why would I hire one of the redskins? I got American boys on my detail. I don't hire the entertainers, anyhow. That's your bailiwick."

"Damn right it is, and this guy's trespassing. Get him out of there."

"Look, Mr. Maxwell—"

"Now!" Maxwell couldn't admit that his ego had suffered a blow. He didn't want to look foolish, didn't want anyone to see that he was hurt that the television cameras had turned away from him. Luckily for him, he didn't have to. He was the owner, the one with the money and the right to give orders.

It made him all the angrier that the other dancers had pulled back to form an appreciative circle around the interloper. They weren't just going through the motions anymore. Now their clapping picked up tempo to match the new man's. They seemed to be remembering something grander, something more sacred, from their past. Even through their alcoholic haze they were able to identify authenticity, and they loved it.

"I told you to get rid of him. He just had a few too many, and he's lousing up the show. Get him off the property so the other guys can finish up and I can get these suckers indoors to spend some money before their buses have to move on."

The security chief shrugged, then turned to the small group of good old boys he'd hired for the day and nodded at the offending Indian. "Let's clear him out."

The men didn't hesitate. They were used to dealing with troublesome Indians in that part of the country. The flab at some of their waistlines didn't mean there wasn't something much stronger and more powerful on other parts of their bodies. Flexing their biceps, they checked the billy clubs that hung from their waists and puffed up their chests. Then the five of them moved toward the outdoor dance floor.

"Come on, boy, time to move on. You're upsetting the audience," Frank Hogan said when he faced the Indian.

"Go to hell," the Indian said under his breath without missing a single beat of the drum or loosing a single carefully calibrated dance step.

Frank Hogan made his first mistake. He put a hand on the Indian's bare shoulder and gripped it hard. He thought he'd done it with enough force to make the guy understand how much more pain Frank could inflict and choose to go quietly. Hogan was used to other men doing that, going quietly.

Instead the Indian threw an elbow into Hogan's belly. The blow was so intense that part of his arm actually seemed to disappear into the security chief's fleshy midsection.

That wasn't what was most amazing to the other guards, though. Nor were they really stunned when Hogan bent over and began to toss his breakfast over the pavement of the parking area. What was really impressive was the way the Indian kept up his dancing.

But aesthetics wasn't the prime issue of the moment. Making Maxwell happy enough to sign their paychecks was much more of a priority for these men. In a group, they moved forward, in the direction of the strange Indian.

The tourists' cameras were clicking at high speed as the possibility of a real confrontation between the whites and the red men seemed to be developing. It was an audience that loved the spectacle of prime-time wrestling. Blood was going to flow, and they had their best chance ever of seeing the real thing, not just the video reproductions.

They were wonderfully rewarded. One after the other the security guards went up against the Indian, and each one was quickly and effectively sent spinning out of the center of the circle.

A punch bashed in the nose of the first guard, sending a gusher of blood spewing out of his nostrils and leaving him screaming with pain as he held his hands over his face.

The next man got a broken nose, as well, but the blow wasn't straight on this time. The Indian's punch landed on the side of the nose and the cartilage simply collapsed to the side, flattening against the man's cheek. The force stunned him so much that he didn't even see the knee coming up to smash into his groin so hard that he could do nothing but melt to the ground and curl up in a fetal position.

The next two guards succumbed to fierce punches in their stomachs. They'd decided to come up to the Indian as a team, giving themselves the best odds possible to face the challenge. But they ended up only providing the Indian with twin targets. Each of his fists landed in their two spongy stomachs at the same time, and they doubled over with surprising synchrony.

That left only one security guard still standing. Clancy Lee was actually the toughest of the bunch, the one in the best shape, and the one who came closest to being brave. He was also smart. Looking around at the figures writhing on the asphalt pavement, he did a quick calculation. Then he checked out the Indian, who was still moving his feet and pounding on his drum while he stared at Clancy with a ferocious look, one that said he was just waiting for the next move.

Clancy shrugged his shoulder, gazed right back at the Indian and said, "Wanna dance?"

ALEX NANOS PULLED into the parking lot of the Osage Arms motel about fifteen minutes later. He got out of the Cadillac he'd rented in Oklahoma City. It had come with all of the refinements. This was no price-buster from Avis that Alex had been dealing with. In addition to the expected air conditioning, there was a cellular phone, cruise control, a radar detector, a compact disc player to go with the stereo, and just about every other refinement possible in an automobile.

Nanos was immediately struck by the blast of hot wind that was blowing off the prairie under a brutal sun when he stepped out of the car's climate-controlled interior. He wiped away the sweat that quickly appeared on his forehead and damned Billy Two for his insistence on coming back to his native state during this last break the team had gotten.

Why couldn't Billy Two be a civilized man and go to Florida for the beaches and the bimbos like anyone else. Or use his huge salary and just rent a luxurious mansion on Malibu Beach on the Pacific and stock it with aspiring movie starlets. It seemed that Billy Two couldn't even consider going to the Riviera and taking a penthouse apartment overlooking the Mediterranean and the beaches full of European beauties who couldn't wait to meet rich Americans. But no, Nanos deduced glumly. Such things were beyond the Indian's ken.

Billy Two had to come home to Oklahoma and get authentic. The damned problem with authenticity was that when it was time to go out on a job someone else had to come and get the newly authenticated person and take him away from hellholes. Nanos kicked the Cadillac's wheels in frustration, sighed deeply with annoyance and walked toward the group that was clustered near the entrance of the new motel.

What did Billy Two have to do with this? Nanos wondered. His friend not only had the huge income that the rest of the SOBs got but was also William Starfoot II, heir to one of the great Oklahoma oil fortunes. Nanos knew that Billy Two could buy and sell a dozen such places without making his accountant blink.

The name of the motel suggested to Nanos that perhaps Billy Two was making an investment. Billy Two was a pure-blooded Osage, and he'd turned his love of his heritage into a fetish. He still claimed he spoke to Hawk Spirit, one of the traditional gods of the warrior nation. Nanos remembered the countless rambling talks about the weird spirit that Billy Two had subjected him to over the past few years. Only the best of friends would have tolerated that kind of thing.

Nanos was at the edge of the crowd but couldn't see much. He didn't care what the demented Osage was up to. It only mattered that it was time to come and get him again. It always fell to Alex to find Billy Two when the call came from Barrabas. In the past he'd had to hire helicopters to ascend tall mountains where Billy Two had been meditating. He'd once had to hike into the most isolated part of Alaska to find the Osage in the middle of the wilderness. He didn't know if tracking the guy down at a tourist trap was any better than that—just a little easier on the travel, not a whole lot easier on the mind.

Nanos cautiously tried to make his way to the front of the group to see what they were looking and cheering at. The women and men all seemed to have a blood lust about something. Nanos figured that if Billy Two was there he must be in a fight. That would never be a surprise. The Osage loved a good brawl as much as Nanos did himself.

But when he got to the front line of the group, Alex saw something he'd never expected. There was Billy Two dancing with some bare-chested white guy. The two of them had worked up a mighty sweat that was falling off their bodies. They were really getting into it, howling ugly sounds and jumping up and down on their feet as though the asphalt were too hot for them to stand it.

Whatever was going on with them, Nanos figured it had something to do with the blood-drenched men writhing on the ground and adding their own decidedly nonmusical howls to the entertainment.

Nanos just shook his head in wonder and didn't attempt to figure out what it was all about. Just another chapter in the life of a friend of Billy Two.

Alex walked up to them and stood with his hands on his waist in front of his Osage pal and waited until the

Indian came out of his trance enough to recognize him.

"Alex!" Billy Two suddenly said. He stopped dancing and didn't seem to notice that his partner was still into it. There were some ratty-looking Indians making sounds on primitive drums along the perimeter, and they had helped Billy's partner really get going.

"We got an assignment, Billy Two. Priority One. Right now. We have to meet the boss in Stockholm tomorrow, at the Hilton. There's a flight out of Tulsa at five o'clock this afternoon that connects with SAS to Stockholm, but it's tight. We have to start moving, now."

"You got it. Let's go. I got my passport and my credit cards in my belt wallet. Always prepared, just like the Boy Scouts." Ignoring the disappointed moans of his fans, Billy Two moved through them, holding Nanos by the arm and asking him where the car was.

"Billy Two! You can't get on a plane dressed like that! For God's sake, that guy's BVDs cover more."

"Oh." Billy Two looked down at his scantily covered body, unaware that dozens of female eyes were making the same trip at that very moment. "Guess you're right. I'll pick up some stuff on the way—jeans, boots, that'll do it."

"In *Sweden*? You need more than that for Sweden."

"Okay, okay! I'll get more than that. Let's go. There are stores everywhere. You said a five o'clock plane. We're going to have to move it. Watch the air conditioning in the car, though, will you? I could get chilled."

"I'll chill you," Nanos said, sneering as he unlocked the Cadillac and climbed in. Billy Two got in on the other side and sat beside Alex. The Osage stared straight ahead, as though he were going to go into one of his religious trances again. Before that could happen, Nanos wanted some questions answered. "What were you doing out there?"

"Damned developers were going to rip off the Osage history to make some sleazy bucks."

"So you were doing your dancing to make their investment worth less?" Nanos asked.

Billy Two smirked. "Oh, no. I bought their investment."

"What?"

"Yeah, they're hocked up to their belly buttons. I picked up the paper from the local bank and gave them a rate that didn't encourage any questions. My lawyer is going to foreclose in about another hour. I was just coming to the 'grand opening' to do the rituals right so I wouldn't have to go through an entire purification ceremony later. It worked. Found me a bro in there, that white-looking guy."

"'White-looking?' I don't get that."

"He's got some Osage in him, enough to let in Hawk Spirit. Good man. He wasn't properly dressed and adorned for the ritual, though, but I didn't have any extras for him, so we made do. We were getting into the music, Alex, really calling up the spirits together. I think I'll make him a manager."

With that, Billy Two picked up the mobile phone that was on the console between them and pushed a series of numbers. He held the receiver to his ear and someone evidently came on.

"Yeah, look, Bowser, there's a guy at that motel I'm taking over. Yeah, on the interstate. Get out there right away and find him, will you? He's stripped to his jeans, and he's dancing with the people. Yup. No, no! I don't want him arrested for trespassing—you're talking about the one we're foreclosing on. This guy, I want him made manager. Give him a good salary, enough to keep him honest. What? Twenty thou? Are you kidding? Make it fifty, with bonuses. And tell him I know he's got to be part Osage if he dances like that, so he should be good to the people, make sure they get some good jobs. I don't care if it's bad business; he's a good man."

With that, Billy Two hung up the phone and sat back in the car with his arms crossed over his bare chest.

"Does that developer realize he's going to be fore-closed on?"

"Nah," Billy Two answered while continuing to look straight ahead. "I had to hire a big-shot lawyer to find the fine print. Any mortgage, there's fine print the bank puts in to screw you. It was there. He's going to lose a bundle, too, the way I got it worked. That'll teach him to try to exploit the Osage Nation."

Nanos shook his head and just kept on driving in silence. He knew better than to investigate any further. He just felt sorry for the developer, who'd probably only made a minor mistake in favor of bad taste, that was all. Now he'd lose his shirt. Well, that usually did happen to anyone who went up against Billy Two. In any arena—financial, physical, military—the Osage was always going to come out on top. It was one of the very best reasons for having him on the team.

Alex Nanos looked at the speedometer and at the clock. Given the way they were going, they'd just have enough time for Billy Two to run into a department store and buy some decent clothes. The Greek included in his calculations the time they'd lose because of the stir he'd cause when the rest of the customers saw him. Then they'd be on their way to New York and, from there, Sweden. He just hoped the rest of the team wasn't having such a trial in making the rendezvous with Barrabas. No one should have the trouble Nanos had with Billy Two. No one.

CLAUDE HAYES KNEW that everybody thought he was a pro football player. People like to stereotype others, he thought, and his physique certainly encouraged that impression.

He supposed it wasn't a bad fantasy for them to have, so he just let it happen. After all, he couldn't just announce to the others in the compartment that he was really a mercenary. That'd go over just great.

He relaxed back into the huge leather-upholstered seat and took a sip of his Scotch. The flight was non-stop from L.A. to Paris, and from there he'd catch his connection to arrive in Stockholm right on time. A few more cocktails, some sweet talk with the pretty waitresses, a good meal, and then he would be ready for a nice little nap to help him pass the time. Sometimes life was so good and so uncomplicated. It certainly had been in Los Angeles.

Claude grinned when he remembered the sweet taste and soft feel of the lady he'd been seeing there. She was a big rock star who was just making it into the movies. She had the big house, the big car and all the

rest of the stuff that went with her big paychecks—
except the big man who knew how to make her happy.
That hadn't come along until Claude had found her in
a snazzy restaurant on Rodeo Drive one night. She'd
been with some overanxious movie producer who was
obviously not the kind of man who knew what to do
with a real woman like her. He might have known at
some point in time, but he certainly didn't possess the
art of holding on to her.

It had only taken minutes after their eyes had met
across the room for Claude and his lady to walk out of
there, and then had followed days when he'd just
sprawled on her satin sheets or sunned himself at the
edge of her pool.

At first she'd been nervous, afraid that he was simply another man after her money; lately, that had
happened much too often to her, just as it would to
any woman who had unaccustomed wealth and no one
to really look after her. Claude had seen the signs, and
he'd done the only thing he could to knock that suspicion out of her. They had gone on an afternoon trip
to the fanciest jeweler in Beverly Hills. An emerald
brooch, a diamond necklace and a few gold bracelets
later, the issue had been resolved to everyone's satisfaction.

That easy way to end a problem was one of the best
things about being a mercenary. The money was good,
and being one of the Soldiers of Barrabas had its own
rewards, such as teamwork and, especially, following
a leader like the colonel.

There were, though, problems with being one of the
SOBs. One was the need to be constantly available. A
single cablegram, and they had to be off and running.

None of them had ever missed a roll call, and no one would do it unless it was absolutely necessary.

Claude had just finished that thought when his meditation was interrupted by an announcement.

"Ladies and gentlemen, this is the captain speaking. Please remain calm. It appears that we have been hijacked. We are being ordered to change direction and to take this plane to North Korea. Our...new superiors would like a word with you about the situation."

Claude was disgusted. What a damn thing to have happen. Before he could really let it sink in, though, a new and scratchy voice came over the loud speaker.

"We are representatives of the All-People's Revolutionary Movement. We've been forced to take this action to escape the fascism of the United States and flee to live in harmony with our brothers and sisters in the People's Republic of Korea. The flight will take some many hours. We're going to use this opportunity to educate all of you about the horrors of American capitalism and the promise of the People's Republic of Korea, hoping that you'll see the light and join us when we land at Pyongyang, the glorious capital."

Glorious capital! Claude Hayes repeated to himself with silent irony. He was one of the very few Americans who'd ever seen what a dump Pyongyang really had become. It made Cleveland look like the garden spot of the world. The climate was cold and harsh, the people were beaten into submission, the most basic foods were rationed, and it was just a horrible place to visit.

The idea of being forced to go to Pyongyang was bad enough, and the idea of missing a roll call for Nile Barrabas was terrible, but the worst thing was the threat that Claude was going to be subjected to hours of radical bullshit rhetoric. That was the most unbearable thought of all.

But Claude knew just what to do in such a situation. He stood up and lifted his right fist into the air in a revolutionary salute. "Let me join you brothers!" he yelled out loud.

Heads all over the cabin turned to stare at the outrageous gesture. Many of the faces that looked at him showed some shock, but there was also an element of seeing their own prophecies fulfilled. If the man was really a pro football player, he was, after all, a union man, everyone knew that.

A skinny young man came through the passageway from the rear compartment, where the coach-class ticket holders were seated in quarters much less spacious than those in the first-class cabin. He looked at the huge black man with wonder. His presence in the capitalists' section of the aircraft was perhaps suspicious, but as with most simpleminded radicals, the fact that Claude was a black brother overcame all other thoughts.

In his hand was a small but lethal machine gun. Claude couldn't place the make, though it was similar to an Uzi. If it had gotten past airport security, it was probably made of one of the new plastics that had first been developed by the Austrians. Their Steyr guns were able to pass any X-ray check and produced a new threat to civilian air traffic since once again the hoodlums were able to get on board even carefully guarded planes and play havoc with the lives of innocent civilians.

"Brother!" the thin man said as he held out a hand. "We welcome you to our struggle!"

"Yeah, sure, bro," Claude said as he took the tiny fist into his own meaty grip and began to press it ... *hard*.

The smaller man opened his mouth to scream when the viselike pressure intensified. He tried to position the machine gun to fire, but Hayes was able to grab it away from him easily. Unlike the hijacker, Claude knew how to use the things; guns were second nature to him. He pointed the muzzle at the man's head and cautioned him to shut up as he continued to increase the pressure. "Now, how many friends you got on this plane, bro? Tell me quick and tell me true, or you're gonna hurt real bad."

To emphasize his point, Claude pressed even harder, and there was the unmistakable sound of bones threatening to pop painfully out of their joints. A low groan of pain escaped from the small man's throat. "Three," he said, forcing the words past his clenched teeth. "Just three more."

"Where are they?"

"One in the cockpit; two more back there. Please let go. Please!"

"Uh-uh, bro. You'll just get all your courage back, and instead of worrying about your hand getting pulverized you'll think you're a hero or something else downright foolish."

Another passenger came up beside Claude and spoke in the same low tones. "I can handle him. I was a Ranger in the Army. I know how to handle this scum."

The man was at least sixty, but Claude could see a trim torso under his suit, and his wrinkled face showed great determination. Hayes thought it over, then shook his head no. "We'll do it together," he said, then turned to his captive. "What's your name?"

"Mason, Tom Mason. Please let my hand go!"

Claude looked annoyed at the repetition. "What's the names of the two back there?"

"Cynthia Gagnon and Michael Brodsky. Please—"

"I know, I know, you want me to let your damn hand go." Claude shook his head at the sad state of terrorism today and then turned to the veteran. "Just let me set this up for you, then you can take over."

Without warning, Claude released the man's hand and at the same time dropped the machine gun on the seat beside him. Then, so quickly that the other man couldn't react to anything but the sudden relief, Claude reached over and took the terrorist's head between his paws. He lifted the guy up and slammed his skull against the bulkhead so hard the hijacker instantly passed out.

"You were in the Rangers, so you must know how to tie some knots and work a gag," Claude said to the oldster. "Do your stuff, friend, and make sure this one doesn't go anywhere or sound any alarm."

Claude got an enthusiastic salute from his helper, proving that in almost any situation one could count on meeting like minds.

Claude moved back to the rear of the plane. He was sure that no one could have seen the little drama that had just been played out. The various partitions dividing the jumbo jet into sections had also obliterated most of the good sight lines. A jumbo jet was a bad choice for hijackers: it was too big, and there were too many people on board.

Hayes could see that when he stepped into the coach section. Families, some of them with small children, were crouched behind their seats, their heads leaning forward against their knees. They'd obviously been ordered into the passive position by their guards, but even a change in posture couldn't have removed their fear, and the soft sobs of the kids filled the cabin.

The sight made Claude Hayes mad.

"Stop! Who are you? Why have you left your seat?" The tall brunette who confronted Hayes had to be Cynthia, and she looked much healthier than Tom Mason had. So healthy, in fact, that Claude was disappointed they were on opposite ends of a machine gun barrel.

"Tom sent me on back here, Cynthia. My bro, he thought I could help y'all." Claude laid the black dialect on thick, just to lend some more texture to his performance. He didn't know if it was that or the seductive smile he shot at the woman that seemed to loosen her up a bit. Whatever it was, it seemed to be working. As he walked toward her, there was no more threat from the gun.

"Why did he do that? What credentials do you have? What group do you belong to?"

"You should know I can't talk about that stuff, honey. You should know what the real underground has to do to survive."

A flicker of excitement crossed her face. "You're in the underground, too! You must be delighted to be going to Pyongyang! They have the most wonderfully socialistic government in the world.''

A shrill-edged voice interrupted the woman's daydreams. ''Cynthia, who's that?'' Hayes deduced that it had to be Michael Brodsky, the third terrorist. The way he flourished his machine gun, he made it look a lot more real and menacing. The man knew how to use his weapon; Claude could sense it instinctively.

Neither the woman nor Hayes answered quickly enough for Brodsky's pleasure. The guy was full of the tension of the undertaking, and the way his head swiveled back and forth whenever a child's cry was heard indicated that he was having trouble dealing with the pressures of the situation.

''Get on the floor! *Now!*'' Not only was Brodsky frightened, he was also mean, and it was a deadly combination.

''Okay, okay,'' Hayes said as he slowly knelt, then lay prostrate on the floor of the aisle between two banks of seats. From his position on the floor, he watched Brodsky's feet come closer.

''Cynthia, how could you let someone do that? Get so close to you? Damn it, this is a military operation. You know our lives are at stake. Bruno's up there with the crew, and there's only the three of us to police this whole— Wait a minute, where's Tom?''

''He was taking care of the first-class section, just the way you told him to. He sent this man back here because he's an ally—''

''Ally? Bullshit. An Oreo, black skin and white inside, one of those drug-using athletes who sell their souls to make commercials for cigarettes to pollute their own people's lungs. How can you and Tom be so naive that you let this kind of jerk get by you with lines like that?''

Brodsky was right by them now, and his attention was being distracted by the anger he was directing at Cynthia. Claude did some rapid calculations. If he jumped the guy first, he risked having a shot go off and pierce the body of the plane. At that altitude, a small bullet hole could rip open a large opening and suck an adult body through it.

A baby's squall reminded Claude that the hole didn't even have to be that large to take a human life.

But he had to do something. He watched as Brodsky stepped even closer to Cynthia. The man kept his gun pointed directly at Claude's head, keeping it ready to shoot if any unexpected moves were made. Brodsky's anger finally provided an opening, though. When he turned his attention on the woman again and continued his haranguing, Claude saw his moment, and he knew it might be the only one.

He tensed his muscles and inched his legs up a slight bit, just enough to give his knees some ability to spring. Then, in one motion, he leaped up into the air, getting hold of the barrel of the gun and yanking it away from Brodsky while with his other hand he grabbed Cynthia's head. As he found solid footing on the floor of the plane, Claude slammed Cynthia's forehead against Brodsky.

The blow staggered both of the hijackers enough to give Claude some time, time he had to use well. He pulled harder on the machine gun, and it came out of Brodsky's grip easily. Holding on to the muzzle, Claude shoved it savagely into the man's gut. When Brodsky fell against one of the chairs and over the armrest into the seat, Hayes continued the assault. After another jab against the terrorist's stomach, Hayes delivered a blow to the chest that was hard enough to cause a distinct sound of ribs cracking. Claude reared the gun back to slam it against Brodsky's head.

A scream pierced the air, but it hadn't come from one of the regular passengers. It had come from Cynthia. Claude not only had to get her quiet, he also had to get her out of commission. A woman with a gun could be just as dangerous as the most ferocious man.

Claude reared back and sent the back of his hand crashing against Cynthia's open mouth, cutting her lips on her teeth and sending her sprawling over the two empty seats beside her.

The entire cabin heaved a silent sigh of relief, but Claude knew the situation was far from being won. One more hijacker was still at large, and he was in the most sensitive part of the plane: the cockpit.

Claude looked around and found what he was searching for. The stewards and stewardesses had been isolated in the front row of the coach cabin. With a cautioning wave of his arm to the passengers, he indicated that he wanted everyone to be quiet.

Claude began to interrogate the flight crew in the front row. As he did, he scanned them with a measuring glance.

Pointing at one of the male stewards, Claude ordered, "You, strip. Right now!" The man, the only one approaching the black warrior in stature, hesitated at the strange order, but then realized that Hayes was peeling off his own clothing in record time.

A buzz came from an intercom. As he pulled off his slacks, Claude told one of the stewardesses, "Get it. The guy up there is going to be freaked by the noise. Say everything is okay and that someone will be there right away to give a report."

Hayes grabbed the steward's slacks and stepped into them. His waist was the right size, but elsewhere the fit would be tight. He picked up the uniform shirt and pulled it on. The biceps were going to be the problem here, and Claude knew the shirt would rip apart the moment he had to flex his arms. He quickly did up the tie and slipped on the jacket, but then pulled it off and ripped it up the back seam. Hayes put the uniform hat on his head and then moved quickly up the aisle.

He got to the door and could see that his helper, the former Ranger, had his prey trussed up. Claude smiled and gave the old guy a thumbs-up. It was just the kind of boost that he needed when he pulled open the door to the cockpit.

The control center for a jumbo jet looks like the computer center for a university. Five crew members were absorbed in carefully monitoring their screens and doing their calculations. Not one of them looked up when the black steward walked in.

The leader of the hijackers was also black. He stared at Hayes through narrowed eyes. "What the hell you doin' up here? What the hell's going on back there?"

"Nothing, man, nothing," Claude said as he stepped into the control area. But this man wasn't going to be so easily fooled. He lifted his machine gun and pointed it right at Claude's belly.

"Not another step. Something's going on, and I want to know what it is. If I don't get a good answer, someone in here is going to become an example."

Claude had to will himself not to tense his muscles. It would end the game right then and there if he did. There was no hope the uniform could stand the stress.

"I made some good contact with Cynthia and Tom, that's all. They wanted me to be the one to come up here so they could keep all the passengers in line. They *trust* me.

"I've been a believer in the revolution since I was in grade school and watched my old man and my old lady get shoved out on the streets of Harlem by a honkie landlord just the week before Christmas. I'm on *your* side, man!"

The gunman seemed to weaken just a bit. He let down his guard only the slightest bit. The gun relaxed in his arms as he thought through what Hayes had just said.

Those seconds of thought and reflection were what did him in. In the midst of all the computer technology that money could buy, while the huge state-of-the-art jumbo jet hurtled through the skies, Claude Hayes fell back on what he knew best—fighting like a man.

There was a screech of fabric ripping apart as Claude's muscles tensed and then sent him jumping forward to land a roundhouse punch directly on the man's jaw. For a split second it seemed that Claude's fist was embedded in the other man's skull. Then the man was lifted up into the air by the force of the blow and just as quickly crumpled onto the floor.

The co-pilot had jumped as soon as he understood what was happening and grabbed the machine gun.

"The rest of them?" he asked Claude while the black man rubbed the torn skin on his fist.

"They're all done in. Everything's just fine."

"Great!" the captain announced from his seat at the controls. "We're going to turn around and head back for the States to turn these criminals in."

"Hey, after all I've done?" Claude said with the tone of someone who wants to win another person over to his point of view. "I'll miss my appointment—a very important one. Besides, we're not that far from our destination." As a last plea, Claude looked the captain straight in the eye and said quietly, "Maybe you owe me one."

The captain looked stunned, then took in the sight of the unconscious gunman sprawled out on the floor. "Well—" the officer beamed at Claude with sudden enthusiasm "—the government might not understand, but I think you're right. On to Paris!"

8

Nile Barrabas stood in the middle of his suite in the Stockholm Hilton and looked around the room. All the SOBs were there, busily catching up on each other's news.

"You should've seen the man," Alex Nanos was saying to Nate Beck, "barely dressed and hopping up and down—"

"I was dancing to Hawk Spirit," Billy Two announced ceremoniously. He was sitting on the couch with his arms crossed over his chest. Nile was sure he saw a glimmer of a smile creasing Billy Two's mouth, but he didn't say anything about it. He'd had the growing suspicion lately that Billy Two was exaggerating the depth of his identity with his Indian heritage to tease the rest of the team. So long as the Osage kept on coming through with the goods, though, Nile wasn't going to blow his cover.

"Hell, Claude, don't you realize that a round of bullets through the skin of an airplane like that could have been lethal. The depressurization of the plane could have..."

"Yes," Claude calmly answered Geoff Bishop. The Canadian was the resident pilot for the SOBs, and he would be concerned about that kind of safety issue.

"I wouldn't have to have done it alone if you'd been on my flight, Liam. Weren't you in L.A.? I thought you were still working on your Hollywood deal with Malcolm MacMalcolm."

The Irishman's eyes turned dark as soon as Hayes addressed him. For the past year Liam O'Toole, the poet of the group, had been trying to get a movie made from his writing. A big-time star-turned-producer had lured him into the brazenly glitzy world of Hollywood and led him through a series of hoops as demeaning and as ego-crushing as the countless humiliations the publishing industry had subjected him to.

"I'd left. I was in San Francisco. There's a woman there—big-time video—a real *artist*, who's interested in my poetry for what it is. She's going to produce a film of it."

"Really, Liam! That's great news," Lee Hatton said warmly. She was the only woman on the team, and its doctor, as well. Her academic credentials and her professional demeanor hid a highly skilled and competent soldier. She was the daughter of a much-decorated veteran of the Second World War, a man who had deservedly achieved the rank of general, and the genes came through in his only child.

"Tell us more about it," Geoff Bishop said. "What kind of track record does this lady have?"

"She's won festival after festival," O'Toole said. "Real art, none of the Hollywood shit."

But something in the way Liam spoke made them all suspicious. He was acting as though there was a secret, and they each wondered silently what it could be.

Nanos was the one of the group who had the fewest compunctions about other people's privacy. "Hey, Liam, you putting it to her? Is that part of the deal?" The Greek's leer was friendly, the kind of buddy-to-buddy thing that he did all the time.

It got an immediate reaction from O'Toole, who blushed furiously. "All creative people—" He broke off his rationalization, then suddenly burst out, "God damn, the woman is strange. She wants me reading my poetry wearing old-fashioned steel armor, like the Knights of the Round Table, and she keeps on saying that to rehearse we have to get to my 'inner self.' Seems that my 'inner self' had to come out wearing no clothes. She has me strip naked and stand there reading while she studies my 'aura.'"

The group cracked up when they heard that. Lee Hatton, who'd never really gotten over her gender's maternal instincts, was the one who tried to be responsive by stifling her laughter first. "Oh, Liam, it always happens to you, doesn't it? This precious poetry of yours is always just something that people use to get something else from you. I'm so sorry."

"My poetry will live!" Liam insisted, blushing all the more while his friends continued to laugh until they became aware that Barrabas was silent. One by one, they assumed serious expressions and turned expectantly toward the man they all thought of as the "colonel."

Nile Barrabas had wanted to get on with the business at hand. He also wanted to avoid Liam being the butt of more jokes because he could sense that Nanos had only begun to produce the digs.

In the momentary silence they individually thought how, deep down, they were awed by the big man. Through countless battles and assignments, they'd seen him stand tall against all odds. His savvy and his ability to plan had brought them many successful missions and had saved each of their lives more than once.

Like all really good soldiers, the SOBs also knew that they had to give in to their leader. There could be no democracy in battle. No matter how strong their individual egos and no matter how adamantly they defended their independence outside the context of the team, they all brought to the SOBs the blind loyalty of the warrior.

The first rule of the warrior is to pledge allegiance to his chief. That was who Nile Barrabas was, and they all knew it. When he began to talk, they listened. It was the way it had always been through their years together, and they knew it would stay that way so long as they were together.

"We're here primarily because Sweden is a neutral country," Nile began. He was standing while the others occupied the luxurious couches and chairs in the penthouse suite. "We're doing something that our allies can never discover. It seems there has been a major embarrassment to our security. Our friends in Washington don't want anyone who is dependent on us to ever discover the recent happenings, and they'd just as soon no one ever found out what we're going to do about it.

"Geoff, are you aware of the Panther air defense system?"

"Sure, Nile, it's the newest thing we have going. It uses the best of our current technology now, but it's set up in such a way that it can become an integral part of our Star Wars defense if that's ever put into place."

"Right, and you understand it well enough to know that it could also be used for civilian purposes as part of an air traffic system."

"Sure, in theory, because the idea of tracking planes is the same, whether you're looking for enemy ones or you're trying to help friendly craft land safely. But the Panther is the biggest thing going in our defense system, and we can't let it be used for civilian purposes because the technology—"

"It is being sold for just those purposes by Continental."

Geoff was obviously stunned by the news. "Nile, are you saying the Pentagon is allowing that technology to get into the hands of civilians?"

"Not only that, the first purchaser turns out to be the Soviet Union."

"Nile, that's as bad as the Japanese and Norwegian sale of the computers that allowed the Soviets to produce submarines as quiet as our own. Those two sales negated a decade's worth of advantage we held over the Russians in underwater warfare. It was a disaster."

"This kind of activity is a constant threat. That's the problem. No one can find out about it, but we have to find a way into the Soviet Union, and then we have to discover the location of the Panther and we have to bring it out."

"Hell, if the Russians know what they have they'll be guarding it with their lives."

"We do have something on our side in all this, though," Nile said, almost to soften the blow. "We have an inside man. There's been a top operative working in the same area as the Panther's new location. The CIA has turned him over to us. They swear by him. His code name is Adonis. He has already located the system, and he'll be there to guide us to it."

"Where?" Liam O'Toole demanded. He was always focused on his job when he was with the team, but in his desire to escape any more scrutiny of the intersection of his personal and literary life, he was even more anxious than usual to get to the bottom line about the operation.

"It's in Riga, the capital of Latvia," Nile said, getting on to the more specific details. "That's Adonis's home base. The Soviets are giving us an unexpected helping hand this time by choosing the one place in their entire empire where we have eyes and ears that we can count on. We have to go in and get it out."

"How?" Liam asked. "After that fiasco with the private plane piloted by that German kid landing in the middle of the Kremlin, the Russians have really stepped up their security."

"There are always weaknesses in even the most sophisticated defense systems, just as that same incident proved. We're undercover as a group of people interested in oil exploration in the Baltic. We have a contact here in Sweden with a private flying service that is going to set us up for an over-the-horizon insertion on the Latvian coast. It'll be up to us to get to Riga overland, where we'll meet with Adonis and get on with it.

"We'll need Nate Beck to help us disassemble the Panther once we get it. It's too large to carry out in one piece, but it can be broken down into components that can be more easily transported with Adonis's help."

Barrabas turned to the computer specialist. "Nate, you're going to have to study the plans of the Panther even more closely. There are large sections of it that are not unique and don't have to be removed from Riga. It's the top-secret guts of the thing that we have to take care of."

"No problem, Nile, I'm already on the case. You're absolutely right, the casing of the Panther, for instance, and the microchips that are part of its operation, are child's play, no big deal. The Russians could have bought that part of the hardware directly on the open market. What's important for us to get out is the heart and soul of the system. It can be done easily, if each of us takes one of the parts that I can divide up without a hassle. It will mean at least four hours of uninterrupted hard work. If you can arrange the time, I can do it."

"Well, this will test Adonis, that's for sure," Nile remarked.

"Who is this guy?" Nanos asked. "The only real operatives I've ever known about inside the Soviet Union have been in the KGB or one of the other military espionage sections of the government. The few dissidents the Russians let live in society almost never have anything worth selling."

"Some of the physicists—" Lee Hatton began.

"Yeah, sure, but they're selling their own inventions and their own experience. The Soviets don't let their scientists know any more about each other's work than is absolutely necessary. Certainly they've never leaked any useful information to us in that way. What usually happens is that the CIA gets them out, and then they spill their guts. But that's damn rare.''

"I don't know very much about Adonis," Nile admitted, "and it doesn't look as though very many people do. He's been able to send a flow of information to Washington that's always proven correct. It has always been the good, meaty stuff, troop movements, fleet operations, the kind of thing that's so important but is too often overlooked in this world of supersophisticated warfare. He's the gleam in the CIA's eye."

"That makes them pretty unhappy about what we're doing."

"Why?" Geoff Bishop asked.

"Because this operation carries with it a very good chance that we're going to blow Adonis's cover. We have to be prepared to bring him out with us. The boys at Langley don't like losing their star. The fact that the powers in Washington have overruled them is one more indication how much they care about this little excursion."

"Cover? Resources?" Geoff Bishop was the one in the group who was most focused on these issues.

"We're going to have to use mainly civilian resources. We're not involving our allies in this, and there certainly are no bases in neutral Sweden or Finland, the other potential staging areas. The plans are very simple. We're going to use our guts and your skills to take on the Soviets, and we're not going to rely on any fancy technology to do it this time. The biggest issue right now is time. The Russians are sure to already be at work on the Panther, taking it apart very carefully and putting their top scientists on it to figure out just how it works. The more days we hang around and look at our belly buttons, the closer they get to working out its secrets. The sooner we're on the job, the more sure Washington can be that the Russians aren't going to retain anything of value to them."

"When do we get into action?" Lee Hatton asked. As the medical doctor, her concern revolved around the team being in top physical condition. Right then, she knew they were all feeling the effects of jet lag.

"Tomorrow night."

There was only a sobering quiet as everyone got into the mood of mentally preparing for battle.

"We meet at dusk tomorrow night. I suggest you all get some rest to make sure you're fully alert by then. We are going to need it."

Barrabas had spoken with the calm voice of authority, which they all found reassuring. "By the way," he added, "it's the usual fee."

One by one the team stood up and moved toward the door. It was going to be a daunting assignment, and they all had looks of determination on their faces.

9

Even in August, dusk brought a chill in Sweden. A latitude that far north meant the shortening of the warm season, especially anywhere near the ocean.

Alex Nanos wondered where and when he'd ever been so cold in summer, and then he remembered a beach house he'd once rented in Bar Harbor, Maine. He'd been told that the women there were not only beautiful but richer than Croesus. It was back in the days when he and Billy Two had been living high and allowing certain women to express their fondness by generous material means, too.

But the summer in Bar Harbor, at the very northern extreme of the Gulf of Maine where it met the mouth of the Bay of Fundy, made for bad business. The usual romantic trysts on the beach after nightfall were out—it was just too cold. Showing off for the ladies during the day wasn't that much easier, since the waters of the Gulf were frigid all through the summer. The only difference between braving the waters in August as opposed to June was the slightly altered blue hue a swimmer's skin took on as the water temperature went through its minute changes. It had taken them a long time to remember the romanticism of a huge fire roaring in the hearth before they got their speed and figured out how to make the women happy.

Nanos had hated the whole episode. Billy Two, with his usual ability to find and nurture the good in impossibly bad situations, had claimed that the experience had been wonderful. He liked enduring adversity, thinking it was the best way to build his manhood.

Maine had been a terrible place to spend an August.

Stockholm was never going to be high on his list, and for many of the same reasons. The wind blowing in off the Baltic, which he could feel even there at the inland airport, was all the proof Alex needed to reach that conclusion.

The team climbed aboard the Lear jet and strapped themselves in for the short flight to Gotland, the Swedish island that had a commanding location at the very center of the Baltic Sea.

They were quiet as the jet's engines revved up, ignoring the soothing sounds the pilot made—the same litany that was intoned in every civilian flight on earth. So familiar that they could translate the words to it even without understanding a word of Swedish. The takeoff and ascent into the sky were easy and passed without incident.

Gotland was close enough that there wasn't any time to get used to cruising altitude, not in a plane as fast as the one they were traveling in. In no time at all, the pilot started the descent.

Visby was the principal town of the island. A small place with only about nineteen thousand people, it was strategically vital to Sweden's defense, given its position in the middle of the Baltic trade routes, and it had been since the days of the Vikings.

As the plane approached the airfield, the SOBs discerned the outlines of buildings in the fading dusk. They could see the massive old fortifications of the Swedish marauders, blunt and graceless compared to the Gothic marvels of France or the Renaissance creations of Italy, but still grand in their scale and in the legends of lost power they signified.

The Lear jet's engines whined as they struggled to brake the craft after they'd landed and then slow it down enough to taxi to the private aviation terminal where the team would make its next move.

As soon as the engines were cut, Nile was at the portal and had it open. He jumped to the ground. Olaf Swenson was there waiting for him, just as had been arranged. The Swedish entrepreneur was clearly nervous. He shook Nile's hand and watched as the rest of the SOBs climbed out of the jet he'd provided for them.

"This way," Swenson said as he began to walk over to the waiting Bell helicopter. It was a civilian offspring of the famed Hueys that had seen combat in Vietnam.

Each of the SOBs took a second glance at the civilian version before they really believed they weren't being sent into one of the hellholes of Southeast Asia.

"We're set, then?" Nile asked Swenson.

The Swede seemed very uncomfortable as he looked from the helicopter back to the group of Americans. "You were going to present me with your pilot's papers," he said in a tone of voice that clearly displayed his hope that the documents wouldn't materialize and the deal would be off.

Geoff Bishop stepped forward and handed a sheaf of official licenses and proofs of competence to the businessman. Swenson obviously knew what was up, and he studied each one of the papers with great care.

"They're fine, thank you," he said when he handed them back to Bishop. But then he turned again to Nile. "I would still very much prefer it if you would take on one of my people as a co-pilot."

"Mr. Swenson, as I've told you, there are four others here who are totally capable of taking over the controls of this machine. Your reputation is spotless, and my pilot's skills are faultless. Your people aren't necessary."

Swenson looked out over the bleak landscape of Gotland and wondered for a moment. He finally voiced his thoughts. "I've never heard of oil exploration in the Baltic."

"You know full well that the biggest discoveries of petroleum deposits recently have been in the North Sea, at just this latitude, and in Alaska, much farther north. We've all had to get over our mistaken fantasy that oil only comes from the desert sand or the tropical jungle. The way things are going in the Middle East these days, any secure oil supply is going to be worth a fortune. You've checked our credentials. You know we've registered with all the appropriate authorities."

Alex looked over at the big Bell helicopter and wondered if they'd have to take it by force. Could they do it? Of course they had the manpower for it, but would the diplomatic repercussions be automatically so heavy that they couldn't risk it? Or was the assignment in Russia so vital that they had no choice?

Swenson didn't make them decide the issue. He sighed and took the cashier's check out of Nile's hand. He'd demanded an eighty-percent deposit, and Barrabas hadn't haggled. His investment should be secure.

"Thank you, and good luck."

They all let out a collective sigh of relief when they watched the Swede walk away. The situation would have been extremely difficult if he'd continued to put up resistance.

"Let's get on with it," Nile announced.

They began to load their gear into the helicopter. As soon as they'd transported everything, Geoff Bishop started up the engines.

The whine of the rotors took them all back, to other countries, other battles.

They were soldiers, driven to that vocation by a need they could never communicate to another person. It was something beyond glory, beyond courage.

The constant womanizing that Nanos did, Billy Two's quest for his spiritual center, Geoff Bishop's solitude in the Laurentians, Liam O'Toole's desperate attempts to have his words become public, Nate Beck's compulsive study of computers, Lee Hatton's careful nurturing of her father's memory in the home they'd shared on Majorca, all of that was simply a way to try to cope with the episodes of civilian life that weren't sufficient to encompass this unique part of themselves, the part that made them true warriors.

As Nile Barrabas looked over his troops, he understood that about them; he understood it better than any one of them did. That was his strength as a leader, to know what they were about, to seek their strengths, to compensate for their weaknesses. And it made his own position all the lonelier.

He couldn't indulge in any of the escapes that were available to the rest of them. A leader's burden is to be in the present, to never let the distractions of life blur his vision. The mission was vital to his life, not just when it was happening, but always. The mission was what Barrabas waited for. Everything else in life was secondary.

Barrabas stood up and moved to a position in the center of the helicopter. The Bell was speeding across the Baltic at treetop level. The phrase was the military term for flying only tens of feet above the surface of the earth, thus avoiding even the most sophisticated radar detection. The Bell's powerful engines were producing such rapid movement of the rotors at that low level that they were leaving a wake in the ocean below as the chopper sped toward its destination.

"Here, Nile, your turn," Lee Hatton said as she passed him the can of camou grease.

Barrabas looked over the group and saw that they looked like apparitions from another world. They were smeared with olive and black streaks of grease, and only their eyes shone out of the camouflage. All of them wore heavy black fatigues as protection against the harsh elements of the Baltic and camouflage against eyes that would expose them.

Nile dipped his fingers into the grease. He smeared it onto his face while the others watched. There was nothing but respect for this painting of the human body. It was a primal rite, as sacred as the war paint of the American Indian and as old as the blue dye the ancient Celts had used to cover their entire bodies before they'd gone out to do war against their enemies.

The mere mortal man had to be transformed before he went into battle. Social historians believed the purpose of the painting of a warrior's body was to frighten his opponent. Modern strategists talked in terms of the value of visual camouflage. Neither had it right.

The paint let the fighter take on a different persona, become *more* than he had been before. It wasn't just the protection the camouflage provided: it was the rite of becoming different, something other, something more, and it always worked.

Nile had seen grown men in Nam cry when the camou had been put on them. He'd seen men weep while they'd prepared for combat, sitting and staring at each other while their fingers had performed the magic of the paint.

It was done. Nile dropped the can back onto the floor and surveyed the team once more, now colored just as they were, now transformed with them. He spoke loudly so he would be heard over the shrill sounds of the rotors.

"We're going in by rubber raft. It's an over-the-horizon insertion, which means we're going to be miles from the coastline. As you know, we didn't have time to get a boat out here, so that's why we're using rubber rafts."

"Zodiac raiding craft?" Alex asked hopefully.

"Nope. Those have aluminum pods that are simply too large to carry on this bird. We have two small inflatables, which are more than sufficient to get us there. How we get out with the Panther equipment is another story. We'll deal with that once we're in Riga.

"We only have the Heckler & Koch machine pistols that Nate handed out. The H&Ks will be all the firepower we need, hopefully. You have two sets of ammo to go with them. I want you to use the subcaliber rounds for now. We'll lose some oomph to the bullets, but the size of the rounds means they won't break the sound barrier when fired, which gives us an advantage almost as good as silencers would have given us. We'll need all the advantage we can muster to get this job done. We don't know what might be waiting for us on that beach. It may only be a case of a lone sentry. If we were to use full-caliber bullets, the sound effects could backfire on us and bring an entire regiment down on our asses before we knew what was happening.

"Your packs also have some special equipment for night fighting. There are Starlite scope goggles. I want you to wear them tonight. There's a moon out, and that's all they need to be able to give you great vision. There are some infrared goggles, as well, just in case we have to use them later on, but you know as well as I do that they're not quite as good as the Starlites.

"We're going to row to a spot on the coast near the small city of Liepaja. We'll have to go overland about a hundred miles to Riga. Adonis knows we're coming in—"

A shocked sound escaped Liam O'Toole. He'd expressed how they all felt. If the operative knew when and where they were arriving, they were at his mercy. If he was a double agent, or if he'd been caught and spilled his information under torture—and they knew that even the strongest man could do that—they could be picked off by the Russians with the greatest of ease.

"He's the best they have in the Soviet Union," Nile said, answering everyone's anxiety. "Because we have to move so quickly, we have to trust him totally. We're going to be put up somewhere in the countryside for the rest of the night. Tomorrow, at dark, Adonis is to get us into the city and show us the location of the Panther. We have to move then. I've said it before, but it bears repeating, we have got to get that machine out of the Russians' hands as soon as possible.

"Geoff's taking this bird back to Gotland, and he'll be waiting for us on a twenty-four-hour basis, ready to come in when we want him, if we can get him a radio message via Adonis."

"We are rather in the hands of this guy Adonis. Have you been told anything about him?" Lee Hatton asked, almost suspiciously. It almost hurt her to think of the superhuman feats they were expecting Adonis to perform. He was an unknown quantity, after all, and yet they had to rely so much on him and on other people's judgment of him. It was a bit disconcerting for the practical Lee.

Nile knew how she must feel and secretly felt just as uneasy. While he could admit some concern, they needed whatever confidence they could muster to give them an edge. "I repeat, they tell us he's the best. I assume, from all the trust they put in him, that he's in the Soviet military. They certainly are convinced that he knows how to use his weapons and his body. I can't imagine any training beyond what he already has to make him any more accomplished—that is, according to the reports."

The group fell quiet, acknowledging Barrabas's words with brief nods that underlined their willingness to trust the colonel. Even when they couldn't be sure of something, what they went with unfailingly was Nile Barrabas's instincts.

The chopper seemed to slow suddenly, and then it was obviously at a standstill in the air. Nile walked up to the cockpit and got a sign from Geoff that they were at the right place for their drop-off.

They'd all been through this exercise in training, and they'd done it enough times in real life. They knew what was necessary. Alex opened the wide side doors of the chopper and was instantly hit by a blast of frigid air.

Liam and Billy Two had taken the inflatables and dragged them over to the door. They were only a few feet above the surface of the water now. The rotors were splashing the cold water all over the place— mainly, it seemed to Alex, directly into his face.

Before Liam and Billy Two tossed their deflated rafts over the side, they secured them to hooks on the floor of the helicopter to make sure the force of the rotor-driven wind didn't send the rafts out of reach. Just as they dumped the heavy loads down into the water, they pulled on a valve that released the gases for inflating the rafts.

The crafts expanded to their full size even before they hit the surface. The team worked with perfect synchrony to get themselves and their supplies safely down to the now-floating rafts. Each of them had two heavy packs, one with weapons and ammunition, the second with survival gear and food and water. Just in case they had to have those things when they hit the coastline or were blown off course.

Alex and Nate Beck had jumped down first into different rafts to load up the supplies and give the rest of the team members a hand when it was their turn to climb down.

It only took a few minutes before they were all on board. The guidelines that had been used to secure the rafts were set free, and the wind from the rotors immediately propelled them away from the helicopter.

Bishop must have been watching and seen that they were all set. The chopper suddenly lifted up into the sky and began to speed away, not wanting to stay in the vicinity to attract any unexpected attention from a stray Russian boat.

The SOBs didn't speak to each other. Putting aside their complaints and worries, they picked up the paddles attached to the rafts. Then they wordlessly leaned into the long and arduous task of rowing against the currents, heading for the coast of Latvia.

10

Nile's Starlite scope goggles had a specific function as the team's rafts approached landfall. The trip had been grueling as the entire team struggled with the currents and winds. They were on the last part of the trip and were about to make their way through the surf. Nile scanned the area. His charts informed him he'd guided the two rafts to precisely the correct location.

The big worry for Barrabas was the Russian border patrols. He knew they'd been humiliated by the Rust flight to the Kremlin, an event whose embarrassment had only been intensified because it wasn't a sophisticated aircraft but a single-engine prop plane that got through what was supposed to be the most complex and airtight air defense setup in the world. They weren't in any mood to have a repeat performance ever in the future.

The Baltic coast was one of the weak points in the Soviet military setup. It had been through that very region that the young German pilot had entered Russian airspace undetected. The barren beaches of Latvia and Estonia were almost impossible for the Soviets to police. The fishing industry of the two occupied republics and of their neighbor, Lithuania, whose shoreline was only a fraction of the size of theirs, meant that the authorities had to let many people out onto the sea under their own power. It was precisely the situation they never allowed to happen on land, where the Russians and their Eastern European allies could—and did—literally seal off access to the West with cement walls, barbed wire, guard dogs and deforested strips of ground that were constantly patrolled by border guards.

But small craft, especially in an area where there were legitimate purposes for their presence, were very hard to defend against. International law made it possible for the Swedish, Finnish and even West German fishing fleets to come precariously close to the coast. The sea was simply too great an enemy, even for the Russians.

Knowing all that didn't give Nile much comfort. He knew he couldn't relax too much or be casual about the abilities of his foes. All it would take would be a single report of the intrusion to bring the might of the Soviet Union down on them.

He kept visually combing the beach as the two rafts tumbled through the breakers crashing on the shore. The Starlite scope goggles should be able to pick it up, he told himself again, continuing his earlier train of thought, when suddenly he spotted what he was looking for.

There, finally, a glow!

The use of a regular flare or even the beam of a commonplace flashlight as a signal would have been too dangerous. Barrabas could now spot Adonis atop a dune as he waved a portable lantern. A filter concealed the lens of the lantern, and only with the special goggles could Nile make out the swinging light.

Nile put a colored sheet of gelatin over his own flashlight, one that in a like manner would make his own signal almost invisible to the naked eye but which should be easily seen by Adonis, who was supposed to be similarly equipped.

The signal was returned just as they made shore. The tired SOBs jumped from their rafts and dragged the craft up onto the sand. Alex and Billy Two, who'd done most of the rowing in their raft, giving Lee Hatton and the less physical Nate Beck a break, sprawled on the ground.

Claude and Liam had to take care of the second raft, the one Nile had shared with them and on which he'd given a more-than-fair share of the labor.

Nile hurried up the slope of the dune, toward the place where he'd seen the lantern. He had his Heckler & Koch machine pistol at the ready. The fear that his contact might have been compromised at the last minute by the KGB was real; he wasn't going to take any chances.

In a while he could make out the outline of a body, thanks only to the Starlite. The man moved toward Nile. When they were almost face-to-face he nodded, then held out his hand in greeting.

"I am Adonis," the young man announced. "My actual name is Janis Valters. I'm your contact, Mr. Barrabas."

THE RAFTS WERE DEFLATED and then had to be buried deep in the sand to make sure they wouldn't be found. Billy Two and Alex Nanos had that task. As tired as they were, they were anxious to get the job done so they could move on.

The rest of the team stood by with Nile and Janis while the labor was completed. The young Latvian was obviously nervous about being exposed on the barren sand. Any coast guard craft or surveillance plane that came along and happened to shine a spotlight on the area in a random check would spot them. Janis wanted everyone out of there.

"Come, quickly," he said with obvious relief when Alex and Billy Two were finished with their task. "There's no vehicle out here. We have to go about five miles to reach the safehouse I've arranged for you inland, and we must do it before dawn."

Barrabas waved to his troops. "Let's go," he said to Janis. "We need a dry spot as much as we need cover. The sea spray soaked all of us through. We're starved after all that work, too. I hope the place you've got for us has some decent food."

Janis simply nodded. Then he began to lead them on their hike through the Latvian countryside.

"A PLACE LIKE THIS reminds me of fairy tales!" Lee Hatton exclaimed when they reached the farm.

Her feelings were shared by the others. The house and its outbuildings were in perfect repair, and there was even evidence that they had been recently painted. While it wouldn't have matched one of the modern spreads in a prosperous agricultural state like Minnesota or Iowa, it had a real charm. Something from a picture book about the "old country" hung about it.

The lights were on in the house. Janis turned to Barrabas and explained, "Not to worry. It is just about dawn, and the family will be up, ready for the chores."

Then he turned to Lee to explain. "Latvia is much better off than most of the rest of the Soviet Union, and these people are able to supplement their income with fishing in the Baltic. With *glasnost*, a bit more free enterprise has been permitted, and it's just this kind of family that's taken advantage of it all."

"Are they your family?" Lee asked.

Janis smiled at the thought, remembering the comfortable bourgeois existence of his civil-servant parents. "No, not really. I only met them a while ago, in fact, through the grandmother. She's one of the old resisters, and she's taught the rest of them well. Come on, they're expecting us. There would have been a sign if anything was off, so we can be sure that it's clear."

Janis led the troop up to the front door of the house. He pulled it open without knocking, and they could all see a family seated at the table, eating their breakfast. They didn't evidence any anxiety about what was going on. If anything, there seemed to be a sense of excitement when they spotted the Americans they obviously had expected.

"Janis! You made it!" An old lady stood up from her seat at the head of the table and rushed to throw her arms around the young musician. The woman appeared to be as close to the earth as any of the SOBs could imagine. She had the full figure of a peasant woman, and her hair was caught up in a homespun kerchief. Her ruddy complexion was proof of the hard work she put in outdoors.

Behind her, a young couple stood up and moved to their new guests. Peteris and Anna Niedra introduced themselves to the newcomers and made apologies for Peteris's grandmother, Elisabeth.

"She has forgotten herself. She always does when Janis is concerned. He saved her life once, not too long ago. The old lady still thinks she's fighting the German resistance," Anna said. "But you are as welcome to our table as he is. Please, come and eat."

Anna got Elisabeth to release Janis, and the two women began to finish preparing the morning meal they'd begun ahead of time. Peteris, who was only about the same age as Janis, in his early twenties, went about the business of being the man of the house. Like the women, he used his English when talking in front of the Americans. Many people in the Baltic States had learned the language in school, along with the required linguistic study, Russian, one they liked much less.

The team wanted to get out of their soaking clothes. They apologized as they stripped down to the essentials, which Anna and Elisabeth quickly set to dry near the stove. Peteris handed them towels, blankets and what robes they had to cover and warm themselves with. When they were more comfortable, he insisted on seating all the SOBs at the table, then on helping his wife to remove the three very young and wide-eyed children who'd just finished their own meal.

The team members dug in. The coffee was strong, the eggs were plentiful, the homemade sausage was well spiced, the fresh bread was as rich and flavorful as good cake.

"Janis saved my life," Elisabeth started, wanting her story told. "I was in Riga, the capital, to bear witness to the rape of my country." As she spoke, her posture stiffened and her voice grew stronger. "First there had been the Germans, and then the Russians. They were both terrible, cruel rulers. Our people have not forgotten that they are in the stranglehold of the Russian Empire, but there is still fear, because too many terrible things have happened. But I don't have that much to lose, and am not afraid to be a public reminder that our free people have become slaves to the Soviet rulers.

"I fought the Germans, hoping that an independent Latvia could emerge again after the war. I blew up railway lines, and slept with those Nazi dogs to get close enough to their desks to find their—"

"Grandmother," Peteris said quickly, "the children will hear you!"

"And let them!" the old woman said with renewed dignity. "Let them know what sacrifices their family made when we fought the Germans, and what sacrifices they will have to make when they take up the cause against the Russians. I wasn't going to let people in Riga forget, that's for sure," the old woman continued bitterly. "I wouldn't hide my head in the sand and make believe that the Republic of Latvia had never been. I went to Knighthood Square with my placards and my banners and I stood there, demanding that the truth be examined and accepted.

"The militiamen came and were going to take us away—those of us who had the stomach to name the victims and point fingers at the oppressors—and label us insane, unfit. They were going to put us away in one of their psychiatric institutes for 'observation.'

"Janis is the one who rescued us. He freed us. I had to seek shelter outside of the city, though, and I came here, to my grandson, to see if he had the family's backbone. He does. He will be one of our new patriotic heroes.''

Peteris wasn't happy with the conversation. Nile could sense that the man's patience was being tried by his grandmother. Not because he was being really embarrassed or upset by her views and her actions—and certainly not by the praise she'd just heaped on him—but because it would only be through an example such as hers that he could fully live up to her opinion of him.

Fear, the daily struggles of living, and hopelessness in the face of such a mighty foe can make people ignore what they can and carry on with their lives. There is a time for heroism, and there is a time when bravery can only be considered foolhardiness, given the restrictions of the odds for success. And sometimes it is difficult to tell the times apart, when to lie low and when to push.

But there were always the prophets of a country who, when they knew the time was right, would stand up and proclaim the truth in a special effort. They made a man look at himself and his life and realize that there were some things that couldn't be denied once the reality had been announced.

Barrabas understood the pain that Peteris was feeling. He understood the conflict the young man must feel because of a natural desire to limit what he saw and felt to this small farm with his healthy children and his attractive wife. And Barrabas knew that once the grandmother had come in and had made the arguments of the generations to him, Peteris had understood his obligation as a man and had accepted it.

That didn't mean he had to like it; it only meant that the decision had to be made. It was like Nile's own understanding of himself. He was the warrior. He had had to embrace that part of himself. It didn't follow that he had to like to hold a gun in his hands and to fire it with consummate skill and kill his enemies. The struggle in life wasn't to be perfect by someone else's standards, but to be honest with who one was.

The team finished the meal. Like athletes before a marathon, they had eaten enough to compensate for their strenuous activity, but not so much that their bodies needed a lot of energy to digest the food.

Of the group, Lee Hatton and Nate Beck were in the best shape, and they took the first watch. The rest went upstairs into the tiny bedchambers, crawling under the handmade quilts and blankets and immediately dozing off.

Nile had never really needed much sleep at all, certainly not when he was on a mission. He'd trained himself long ago to fall into a very deep sleep and to wake up after a short time more refreshed than most men would have been after eight hours.

True to form, his eyes popped open after only two hours' rest. He carefully got out of the bed and walked softly out into the narrow hallway. He saw that Claude, Alex and Billy Two were all still getting their rest.

Barrabas was disinclined to get more sleep. He felt very fine-tuned, with a calm but tautly strung sense of balance, strength and attention. He went down the stairs to check the rest of the house. Lee Hatton and Nate Beck were alone with Janis in the kitchen. They were checking some gear, but it was obvious that the strain of staying awake was getting to the two SOBs.

"I'm up and rested. You two go on, get some sleep."

There was no argument. Lee and Nate didn't even speak as they stood and immediately went up the stairs. That was simple proof of their profound fatigue.

"Some coffee?" Janis asked. "I just made a new pot." Nile took him up on the offer and got his dried-out clothes off the stove, then got dressed while Valters went about pouring the mugfuls of the fresh brew and filling Barrabas in on the happenings around the house.

"Peteris is out in the fields. So is Elisabeth. Anna, though, wanted to take the children over to her own mother's. There won't be a problem; she was simply being protective. The children have been told that you are friendly fishermen who needed a place to stay. They don't understand English, and they couldn't have followed any of our conversations, so the tale will stick."

After handing Barrabas his coffee, Janis sat down at the table while following the other man's restless movements around the kitchen. Restrained energy, the young Latvian thought as his eyes met the American's level and calmly forceful gaze.

"Let's go over the plans. Things like time, transportation, method of concealment," Barrabas said.

"We will have to move into Riga at nightfall. I've arranged for a truck that will allow us entry to the city. There are no guards at the limits anymore; there haven't been for some time. We'll cover the back of the truck with produce from Peteris's farm. The truck isn't traceable. It was brought over from Poland as part of a smuggling scheme that backfired. I was able to track it down via rumors. I've found plates and have some doctored papers for it. The job was done well enough that no one would suspect the forgery."

"Where is our location in the city?" Barrabas questioned.

Janis looked at Barrabas for a moment before he spoke. "The object you want is in the Naval Institute by the waterfront. I was talking to your technical man, Beck, and he said he needed a few hours in order to disassemble the machine and take out the parts you need. That's going to be a big order. I thought you'd just destroy it."

"It's an option. If we need to do that, we will. But the optimal result is taking some of the guts of the thing out with us."

"It will make the whole operation more... challenging," Janis said, "but it will be difficult for your people to live up to your superiors' expectations."

"How are we to get out?"

"I have three different routes prepared for you; all three involve fishing vessels. It's the only hope. I will stay with you and guide you after the operation. Just as a precaution, when we get to the Naval Institute I'll hand you the plans, written on paper, in case we're separated or something happens to me. I won't commit them to paper, though, until we're there. I don't want to risk having my people uncovered if any of you are captured beforehand."

"Understood," Nile said. "You must be pleased with the possibility of getting out of here."

Janis seemed startled. "I'm not leaving."

"But you have to. There's no way you can accomplish all this and not be exposed yourself."

"It's a risk that I must take," Janis said sternly.

"Our leaders were adamant that you have the chance to leave Latvia. It was to be part of your reward. They said they had everything set up for you."

"They never had my agreement because this is certainly not something I've asked for." Janis was getting visibly angry. "I am a patriot of Latvia. I have no desire to emigrate from my homeland."

"You don't want to come to the United States? To leave the Soviet dictatorship? To have the chances that you would get to collect America's gratitude?"

Valters slammed a fist on the table. "I'm sick and tired of my country being used as a tool between the superpowers. I am not doing this for American gratitude! I am doing this to strike a blow against the country that is occupying my homeland. If you were British or Swedish or... I wouldn't care if you were Tasmanian! I would do this to strike against the Russians. If *America* were the occupying force, I would ally myself with the Russians for the same purpose in the same way. I am in this for my people's survival as a nation, not for your ideology."

Nile had taken the measure of the man and was pleased. "I understand. My priority is getting the job done, but if need be, don't forget you have that option to leave. I know—" he paused for emphasis "—that your cause is here."

"If my activities are discovered, and there is no choice," Janis agreed, "I will have to go with you." There was only despondency in Valters's voice. It was clear to Barrabas that the prospect wasn't one that Janis looked forward to.

"There hasn't been a viable resistance movement inside the Soviet Union in decades, certainly not one that we've ever made contact with, nor one prepared to make an armed stand against Moscow. We've only had the refuseniks and the dissenters along lines of art and ideology, and they were always so isolated individually that they seldom could get together to create an organization. What's so different about you? What's going on here that makes you so different than the rest of the Soviet Union?"

"As I've said, it is a matter of national pride, but essentially, beyond that, it is a matter of survival. Latvia deserves and has the need to be a free and independent country. There are many other national groups that feel the same way about their homelands. The Tartars recently demonstrated in Moscow, announcing their craving for more autonomy. The Armenians want their own country.

"The West forgets that this is a new Russian Empire, one that is out to conquer and actually obliterate the many national groups inside its borders. The movement from Moscow is pervasive, with constant attempts to make Russian the official language of the entire Soviet Union and to make the collaborators with the Communist regime ashamed of their native tongues and their native institutions. But the campaign—this 'Russification'—is hateful to the rest of us. We will fight it with everything we have, for as long as we can."

"Yes," Barrabas said quietly. "We have some principles we agree on."

11

Julijis Stucka walked proudly into the situation room at the Naval Institute. The chamber had been set aside as the brain center for the top-secret operation being carried out under his protection, something that gave him immense satisfaction.

Julijis snapped his gleamingly polished boots together and delivered his smartest salute to Nikoli Geogi. The Russian official looked up at the Latvian militiaman with undisguised boredom. "Yes, Captain?"

"You ordered me to report to you, Comrade," Julijis answered, unable to keep the hurt tone of voice out of his response. His greatest hope in this assignment was to impress Geogi, and that didn't seem to be happening if the Russian couldn't even remember the direct order he'd given him.

"Yes, yes," Geogi said, wiping fatigue from his face. He'd been poring over the plans for the Panther that had been coming from the technical investigators. They were still indecipherable. Whatever was inside that damn machine wasn't something that the top Russian engineers could figure out.

The going had been especially slow because they'd had to protect against any fail-safe devices in the equipment. The Americans might have constructed something that would cause the delicate inner workings of the system to self-destruct if approached in the wrong way. The Russians had discovered, much to their chagrin, that much of the American military computer software they'd stolen at other times had been developed with just such a "bug."

As soon as it had been loaded into a Soviet computer and it had been discovered how the software could be accessed, it also came to light that unless a certain command was issued, the software would erase itself automatically. Or worse, it would deliberately malfunction, but in a devious manner not discernible to even the sharpest mind until it was much too late and the illegal operators had already committed themselves to a strategy or operation that would automatically fail.

None of those things could happen with the Panther. It was the coup of Geogi's career to have gotten the highly advanced system from the Americans. Once his scientists were able to get into the machine, they would be able to pull it apart and learn enough to allow them such an advantage that it could turn out to be the means to counter the Star Wars setup that had become so important to the American President.

The painstaking pace of the operation was definitely getting to Geogi, and with its pressures his tolerance of the provincial militiamen who were too anxious to please was fast eroding.

"Your plans for the defense of the Naval Institute are wholly unsatisfactory, Captain. You've loaded the place with militiamen—"

"As you ordered, Comrade!"

"I wish you'd remember to address me as *general*, Captain. The fact that we're both Party members doesn't alter the difference in our military rank."

"Of course not, General Geogi," Julijis said, feeling the reprimand as though it had been a physical blow.

"I had ordered you to secure the institute, of course I did. I had also commanded you to make the defense unobtrusive because I didn't want any special attention brought to the complex. Your so-called undercover operatives are as obvious as they would have been in uniform. They salute you every time you walk by, for instance. Now, Captain, how often do carpenters, plumbers and housepainters salute a member of the Latvian militia, may I ask?"

"I hadn't realized that was happening...."

Geogi took time out for a scornful glance that clearly indicated he didn't believe Captain Stucka. "You people with your pretensions, you're the bane of the entire Soviet Union. You just didn't want to go without the acknowledgment of your men. And for that small, infinitesimal crutch to your ego, you've put an operation with international consequences at risk! Get your men into effective operating stances, Captain, and do it immediately. While this operation lasts, neither you nor they are ever to be military in your bearing or in any manner tip off to anybody watching the presence of this security force. Leave the show to the naval guards who are supposed to be here, who won't arouse any suspicion."

"Yes, General." Julijis snapped to attention once again and turned with military precision to leave the room in a formal march.

As soon as he was out in the hallway and out of Geogi's sight and hearing, Julijis slammed a fist into the wall. Damn the Russian! Stucka knew he deserved better treatment. Again he went through the entire litany of sacrifices he and his family had made for the sake of the Soviet cause. He knew that Geogi was being unfair, that he was letting his obnoxious Russian nationalism interfere with the way he was dealing with the local constabulary.

Julijis could just imagine what kind of report Geogi was going to file on him. It would have every possible slight built into it and make him look like a bumbling provincial, not somebody Moscow would consider for the kind of post that could lead to a major career advance.

He would have to prove himself in some spectacular way if he ever hoped to get anything major out of the situation.

Just as Julijis was thinking through his options, Sophia Nassan, the general's woman, appeared, coming up the corridor toward the situation room. She was hardly young anymore, but her exotic good looks made that irrelevant. She was more than handsome, and her sophistication showed through every pore of her body.

"Comrade Julijis," she called by way of greeting, and smiled at him. She had her usual melting effect on him, just as he knew she had on almost every man with whom she came into contact.

The rumors about her had flashed through Riga as soon as she'd arrived to join Geogi. In her own time she'd been just as famous as he was now, one of the great intelligence gatherers for Moscow, the beloved Mata Hari of the Russian spy system.

Just what she had done, where and under how much control by Geogi was all speculation, but she had earned a special place in the bureaucracy, and she showed it.

The sable coat she wore even on cool summer days was only one of the ostentations of privilege with which she displayed herself. The car and driver—two perks still available only to the most senior officials in the Soviet Union—and the suite in the best hotel in town confirmed the impression that she was someone who held high status in the Soviet world, or else the the man who kept her did, which often amounted to the same thing.

The Russians prided themselves on the rights they had given to women, allowing them to take a major role in the medical establishment, for instance. But Soviet feminism frequently only amounted to an equal opportunity to work for the glory of the communist state, and in high places, places of power, the labor that women were often required to perform had more to do with the bedroom than any practice of authority.

She walked past Julijis—who'd had to restrain himself from saluting her as he tried desperately to follow Geogi's orders. Then she disappeared from sight, and he was left only with her scent, as mysterious and as compelling as her dark olive skin.

That kind of woman was one of the ultimate rewards in the Soviet system, the kind of thing that Stucka wanted badly for himself. He was reacting physically to her presence, demonstrating her potent attraction, and he thought dreamily that he would have had her right there on the floor of the Naval Institute if it had been within his means.

But Stucka knew that women weren't simply a reward, not always. At times they could be the way of achieving a reward. It was time for him to check in with some of his contacts. To adequately protect the Naval Institute during the current top-secret activity would be a good point in his favor, but it would be all the more impressive to discover whether the operation was endangered and stop any trouble before it could happen.

He would have to make sure that Riga was as secure as possible, and he knew where he could start to judge that very element in the situation.

"Nikoli," Sophia said as she walked into the room unannounced.

Geogi gave the beautiful woman no more kindness than he had shown to the Latvian militiaman. "I wasn't expecting you just now," he said, his irritation obvious.

"I forgot that seeing me has become such a bore for you, Nikoli."

"Don't start on that now, Sophia." As her scent assailed his nostrils, he looked her up and down appreciatively. "But on second thought, since you're here, we can at least spend some time together." His tone wasn't conciliatory, though: it was loaded with meaningful innuendo.

"I didn't think...I hadn't come here for that. I thought we might have lunch together."

"But, darling, there isn't time for that. There is time for something else, however. Come, your coat will do perfectly for a bed."

"Nikoli! Please! This is my best—"

Geogi ignored her objections and took off the fur. He quickly spread it on the floor and then began to undo his slacks. "I told you, I haven't much time. Don't bother to undress. Just slip out of your panties and lift up your skirt."

Sophia looked at him with abject defeat. There didn't seem to be any end to the kind of humiliation he would put her through. If she objected, she knew what would happen. He would probably become violent. That was usually his response when he detected a lack of enthusiasm on her part. Or he'd resort to degrading her with his horrible words, some of which she knew were coming in any event.

He was ready and waiting for her with a queer little smile on his lips. She didn't object this time, but went through the motions of doing what he'd asked of her. When the panties had come off, she lay down on the soft fur and spread herself for him.

He didn't waste any time on preliminaries, but quickly and brutally entered her. "Ah, my lovely whore," he said into her ear. It was the part she loathed the most, the litany of dirty talk he seemed to have to have whenever they had sex. "My lovely, expensive whore who would sell anything for money and power. The high-priced prostitute who is available for any assignment, so long as the rewards are high enough."

He kept up that line of talk, driving her mind far from any hope of her own sexual enjoyment while he continued to work intently at his own pleasure. He used her as though she were an inanimate object without feeling and sensation, and whose only purpose was to bring him pleasure.

As soon as he was done, he unceremoniously lifted himself off of her and immediately went about putting his clothing back together again.

"That was an unexpected pleasure, my dear," Nikoli said as he returned to the diagrams on his desk. "But you must go now and leave me to this. I'll be back to the suite for dinner, at eight, I think. Make sure the kitchen comes up with something better than the local sausage again. They may think it's satisfactory, but I don't. The damn manager must have a decent cut of meat hidden away someplace. Make sure he finds it. I know you have your ways of doing that."

Geogi smirked with the last comment. From then on he paid no attention to Sophia, who staggered to her feet and retrieved her underwear. She made herself presentable as best she could. Her purse held a brush, which she used to put her hair in order. Then she smoothed her good dress. Geogi was back over his papers, expecting his curt orders to be fulfilled without argument.

Sophia was a woman who had once been as familiar with the feel of a pistol as she was with the grip of her brush. Her hand groped inside her purse in a reflexive move. There was no weapon there. If there had been, would she have dared to use it?

He was, she reminded herself, the man who had saved her from a Turkish prison. He had sent in the commandos to free her from that wretched existence and to bring her back to Moscow, where she had been greeted as a hero and given all the privileges possible in the capital.

There had been a price to pay for all of that, and the cost was astronomical. It couldn't be measured in terms of money or houses or vacations or the glamorous life of a socialite who regularly attended the most chic diplomatic parties. The cost was carved out of her body and out of her dignity.

Could she shoot him? She wondered about it once again. It had been on her mind for years now. Did she owe him so very much? The cost in self-respect was so great that she questioned if it was really worth giving it up to protect her life. Or was her life just too much for her to bear?

She pushed aside the question, as she had done countless times over the past few years. She couldn't answer it, and she was perhaps too frightened to look any more deeply. Because there was another question that plagued her: if Nikoli decided he wanted a younger, even more beautiful woman, would she be able to retain anything at all? Would there be even a cottage for her in the country?

She knew too well just how powerful Geogi was. He could erase everything in her life as easily as he had created the comfort she had grown used to. He had finessed her out of her position in the intelligence apparatus a long while ago. He'd claimed it was to give her a well-earned vacation, a reward after her sacrifices in Turkey. In fact, it had left her even more vulnerable to him, taking away her independent income and her continued presence in the eyes of the other Soviet spymasters who might have been willing to come to her rescue.

Since then, she'd become utterly subservient to Nikoli, a status he loved her to have. His view on the matter seemed to be that a personal servant doesn't question the master's desires but fulfills them unthinkingly.

Let her elegance and her style be on public view. It made him feel good to see the way they were jealous of what he had at his whim, and he did have her whenever and however he wanted her.

Incidents like the one in his office weren't the only way he took her. More often their sex was dramatic, in the finest beds, on top of the grandest satin sheets. He only made her perform in these horrible ways occasionally, just often enough to remind her that she had no choice in the matter.

Sophia walked out of the office and down the wide corridors of the Naval Institute. The few navy guards saluted her as they watched her leave. The driver was waiting to open the car door for her when she came out of the building.

She climbed into the back seat and wondered about the best way to get the proper kind of meal out of the hotel manager. It was her duty, her job, and she should do it as well as she could. There was no choice. She watched the streets of Riga go by as the car moved away from the Naval Institute. There was no choice, she reminded herself once again.

Had there ever been?

"WHAT DID HE SAY TO YOU?" Koren demanded as soon as Julijis entered her apartment.

Stucka wasn't about to admit the way he'd been treated by Geogi. Not to her. "He admired my plans for the defense of the institute," he announced, "and made some suggestions for further security measures."

"Will you get it? The promotion?"

Julijis looked at the young musician and saw the determination in her eyes. He knew that the only way he could ever satisfy her lust wasn't through anything he did with her in bed: it had to come from his career.

"Of course I will, but the project must be completed before anyone can think in those terms. This is a beginning, and we can't be too greedy now. We must do the work and do it well. Then the rewards will follow."

Koren accepted the answer. She was certainly willing to allow for hard work, which was the most important aspect of her life. She wanted out of Riga, into Moscow or Leningrad. She wanted desperately to leave behind the sham of being a rocker so she could study her beloved classical music. She'd agreed to the role of being a member of the Riga underground music scene only because Julijis had demanded it of her, saying it was the only way that he could really get ahead.

He needed her eyes and ears in places that no member of the establishment could ever go. She'd come through, without ever ceasing to complain about the trials she had to go through while she masqueraded as the lover of Janis Valters, the effete musician who loved nothing more than to be a thorn in the side of the Latvian militia.

Stucka had found the situation an amusing foot-note to his relationship with Valters. After all, when he'd been a snot-nosed brat the kid had followed him around like a little dog. He'd tried to emulate every possible action and attitude that Julijis took, think-ing he'd like to grow up following the older boy's footsteps. Now, just to prove his own superiority over Janis, Julijis had even set up his girlfriend as a plant in the kid's strange life.

"What do you know about the goings-on in Riga's dark underside?" he asked.

"Janis is his usual boring self, full of great artistic statements about the Latvian people and their need to become even more free."

"When this phase, this *glasnost*, is done with, we'll be able to deal with malcontents like him as they should be treated. You're doing invaluable work by documenting just how subversive they are. When the time comes, we can take your information and end this rot in the very center of the country."

Julijis meant most emphatically what he'd said. Actual danger to the state shouldn't be the only con-cern of the militia, and safety not the only thing for it to enforce. The smooth running of the Soviet Union demanded that there be more to it than that. To his way of thinking, it was paramount that there should be discipline and responsible attitudes among the people. His sense of the place of the military and the militia was offended by the thought that civilians could flaunt their disrespect openly on the streets of the Latvian capital.

"I hope it doesn't take much longer," Koren said as she moved across the room to wrap her arms around

Julijis. His strong words had had their usual effect on her. "I hate being among them. Trying to curb them is second nature to me, but I must be so careful, say only gentle things and warn them when I would much rather they were quickly and effectively handled by you."

She leaned into him and kissed him on the neck. "Tell me what you're going to do next to protect the installation."

Julijis recognized this step in their interaction; it was a form of foreplay for Koren. As he began to speak, he could feel the desire rising up inside her. The talk of militia operations was her greatest aphrodisiac.

"I'm going to post extra guards around the city limits, just in case there's some attempt at infiltration. The border patrol is doubling their presence on the coastline as an extra precaution. I already have more than a hundred men surrounding the institute, and the navy has its usual complement of twenty uniformed guards, as well. The building is an impregnable fortress, and it will stay that way so long as the need is present. When it's done, when Geogi is satisfied and has left Riga, then I'll be recognized as I should have been all along. Finally my work will be valued as it should be. My future will be secure."

His immediate future was secure already—he could tell that by the way Koren's hands were moving, first down over his chest, then below his belt where the proof of his own excitement was waiting for her discovery.

12

The old truck bumped its way over the back roads of the Latvian countryside. The SOB team was hidden behind sacks of potatoes and rutabagas.

Nanos scowled. "Not exactly the kind of stuff I'd want for dinner."

"With the money we earn from this," Claude Hayes answered, "you'll be able to buy yourself a year's supply of moussaka. Just think of all that eggplant, all that garlic, all that cheese."

Just then the truck hit still another bump in the road, and they all were tossed around. They endured it stoically, having endured far worse on their missions.

"Don't worry, Alex," Billy Two said, refusing to alter his stiff posture to compensate for the discomfort of the ride. "Hawk Spirit is pleased with this assignment. He thinks it's noble. He likes the young Latvian."

"Great! Just what I needed to hear, that your loony spirit thinks this hip guy is the cat's meow." The Greek's voice dripped with sarcasm. "That's just wonderful. I can't tell you how pleased I am."

Billy Two refused to rise to the bait. "You should be. His pleasure is a good omen."

"What kind of life have I let myself in for?" Nanos moaned.

Just then the truck seemed to come to a sudden halt. All of them reached for their H&Ks, ready for any trouble.

"There's a spot check up ahead—militia. I don't understand it. The traffic into Riga is never searched." Janis's whispered voice came through the partition between them and the truck's cabin.

"Take it easy," Barrabas answered. "Hopefully they'll just check those papers you said were in such good shape. If that's all, we'll just keep on moving. If they want any more, then we'll have to deal with it."

"Okay."

Barrabas noticed the calmness in the guy's voice and relaxed himself. He respected the younger man and his commitment to his cause. If anyone could get them through this unexpected problem, Nile suspected they had the right man at the wheel to do it.

The truck was in a line of vehicles, and it had to stop and then advance as each one was checked out. They couldn't see behind them, but they had to suppose that there were more cars and trucks stacking up to their rear. It was strategically a terrible situation for them to be in. Any escape route was blocked. It was going to be a case of guts and grit, because there couldn't be any fancy maneuvers to get them out of a fix if one developed.

The H&Ks were in hand and ready. The machine pistols were still loaded with subcaliber rounds. That might be the only thing they had going for them. These bullets lacked the distinctive crack of a bullet that was moving faster than sound and wouldn't give them away. But there was no guarantee that they wouldn't be spotted and identified, and any hope of a cover would be destroyed.

The truck lurched forward one last time. "This is it," Janis said through the partition.

There was the sound of Latvian being spoken in front. The team members followed Nile's hand-communicated signals and readied themselves. The H&Ks were seemingly aimed at the sacks of vegetables that separated them from outside, but each one of them was ready for a real enemy. The tension increased and could be almost felt, like a vibration in the air.

A sudden burst of light appeared between the top of the sacks and the roof as the truck's back door was opened. They heard talking again as the soldiers evidently asked Janis some sharp questions.

If the sacks were moved, they all knew what they would have to do. Instead of hesitations, there would be concerted action. The best is what they were trained to give, under any circumstances and against any odds.

The top sacks were being dragged down and tossed onto the ground. Nile aimed his H&K at the slat of light that was showing, waiting for the first man to show himself. The sacks continued to be pulled off the pile. If that routine continued, there would only be a few seconds before they were discovered. Should they wait or should they take aggressive action and make sure they caught the militiamen off guard?

The choice was taken out of their hands. One of the unseen guards yanked at an entire stack of sacks, leaving Nile instantly exposed and staring right into the militiaman's face. The guard was startled, and Barrabas wasn't going to waste that wonderful advantage.

The machine pistol spat out its rounds, bursting its bullets on the man's face, wiping out his features as the rounds pounded against him. Death was immediate. The man was thrown backward and sprawled lifeless on the ground.

The shooting was the only signal the rest of the SOBs needed. Nanos kicked at the pile of sacks that was still in front of him and sent them flying outward. They toppled another militiaman and sent him reeling, just as shocked and surprised as his mate had been.

Claude Hayes jumped through the opening that Nanos had created, and his weapon began its deadly business. There were two guards left standing, and each of them took a dozen bullets in his chest. Hayes's aim was so good and his foes were so unprepared to actually find live contraband in the truck that they never even got a single shot off before they tumbled onto the pavement.

Claude quickly altered his aim and took sight at the remaining soldier on the ground. Hayes had seen the look of shock that came to a foe just as he understood he was a dead man. It didn't make it easier for Hayes to see that expression on a man's face, but it also didn't change Claude's duty. He fired at the prone figure and saw life leave it forever.

Suddenly the SOBs realized that they had another surprise coming. The car directly behind them was a police vehicle. The two men in the car had been given precious seconds that they were able to use to get themselves ready.

Throwing open the front doors, they crouched behind them, using them as shields. They weren't resorting to fancy tactics to make their weapons any less noisy. Their AK-47s were standard issue for all the Russian military and constabulary. The automatic rifles were awesome weapons against any enemy. The SOBs knew that and had nothing but respect for the damage the AK-47s could do.

Claude Hayes was the one closest to the edge of the truck. He saw the AK-47s getting ready and knew he didn't want to be a stationary target for that kind of firepower. He jumped off the truck bed and hit the ground running. Hayes grabbed Janis as he jumped, sending the young man spiraling away from the vehicles with him. The two of them were by the side of the car before the security police could understand what was happening. Their automatic rifles were still aimed at the truck, dispatching a stream of bullets that blazed a pattern against the metal and chewed up the vegetable sacks.

Hayes had his H&K in his free hand as he threw Janis to the ground, out of harm's way. He could see the two policemen through the open doorway of the car. He lifted up his machine pistol and began to fire at them, aiming right for their vulnerable heads.

The man closest to him slumped over almost instantaneously. The bullets from the H&K had cut open his temple, sending a river of blood from the severed artery spewing onto the ground. But the other man escaped Claude's shots. He was a smart man in battle, one who understood that this was a time not for the niceties in life but for using whatever resources he had available to him for his own protection.

The policeman had climbed back inside and had taken hold of his partner's collar and lifted him up, using him like a sandbag to protect himself from Hayes's fire. His AK-47 spit out a long round at Hayes and forced the American to back off and seek cover in the bushes along the side of the road.

That allowed the policeman to lean over and aim at the truck again. The barrage of bullets he and his partner had sent into the back had opened up most of the few remaining sacks, and they'd spilled out onto the roadway. The other SOBs in the truck were going to be open targets for him unless Claude could divert his attention, thereby giving the team members a chance to cut him down from the front.

The situation was getting pretty scary. Hayes kept trying to get a decent sighting of the man, but there was only the barrel of his rifle visible now. Even the man's hands on the trigger were out of Claude's view.

The bullets that the SOBs were sending in waves across the police car hadn't hit the man, but had sent the glass window of the car splintering in all directions. The webs of cracks only gave the policeman more cover, lending a kind of opaqueness and dimness to the car's interior.

Then, out of nowhere, something ended the shooting from the car. The barrel of the AK-47 had disappeared. The SOBs continued to send their fusillade pouring from the truck, but Hayes was the only one who understood that there was no target there anymore.

"Hold it!" he yelled out loud to the rest of them. One by one the nearly soundless subcaliber rounds stopped completely, and there was a silence.

Claude crept around the back of the police car, his H&K ready to be fired if there was anything unexpected going on. When he got to the other side of the vehicle, Hayes saw the policeman, but there was no need to fire his weapon. The man was very dead.

Janis had gotten there first. Evidently he'd crawled directly under the car and had been able to reach the other side without being observed by anyone. He'd taken off his belt and used it as a noose, throwing it around the policeman's neck and drawing it tight to wrench the man out of the car and then strangle him effortlessly when he was on the ground, already partly unconscious.

The dead man's face was bright red from the blood that hadn't been able to drain from the brain. The blood would soon drain away to leave the skin the sickly pale green that was the mask of death. But Claude knew that it wasn't the time for him to mourn the passing of an enemy. He had to make sure the team wasn't in any other danger.

Hayes saw that Billy Two and Alex Nanos were following Barrabas's lead to check out that very thing themselves. They'd stolen out of the truck and were cautiously making their way to the front, not knowing yet if more armed guards were waiting there for them.

"There's no one else at the checkpoint!" Janis cried out. "These two were the only ones behind us. Quickly! We have to get them buried, out of the way, and we must hide this car, too. We have to get into the city before anyone finds this mess."

The car was a ruin from the rounds it had taken from the H&Ks. Only the position of the gas tank in the rear had kept the vehicle from exploding after the amount of molten lead that had been poured into its chassis at such close range. There was no way the engine could be started; the controls had been shattered by all the fire they'd taken.

There were stands of trees surrounded by thick bushes all along the roadway. Following Janis's lead, the team got behind the police car and pushed and pulled the dead metal weight as far into the cover as they could. They all had survival knives as part of their kits, and they were handy for hacking away at some of the vegetation to provide cover for the hulk. The bodies were thrown far back into the bush. After a matter of minutes of hard work, the whole of it seemed to be perfectly camouflaged.

They emerged back onto the road and the next order of business: trying to get the produce back onto the truck fast enough and carefully enough that it could once again provide the team with protection. When the last of the sacks were ready to be loaded, most of the SOBs had to climb in behind them. Nile stayed outside with Janis to do the last of the loading.

Plenty of debris still littered the road, but there was no way to clean it up. They'd been lucky so far that no other traffic had come along, even after the loud sounds of the AK-47s, which would have served as an alarm if anyone had been in the vicinity.

"We're still miles from Riga," Janis said. "We're lucky they didn't establish this roadblock closer to the city itself. We could have been in real trouble if they had."

Barrabas had climbed into the front seat beside the young man, and he looked at him closely. He saw something on Janis's face that was familiar, something he was used to seeing on only the most experienced and seasoned troops.

It wasn't that Valters was exhilarated by the battle, because he hadn't actually enjoyed it. That would put him in the category of a simple sadist. Nile knew that look; he could have spotted it from miles away. Nor could he detect fear or disbelief, the emotions that usually clouded the amateur.

It was more than just the knowledge that a needed job had been done, though. Janis showed a sense of pride that it had been done well. He was in command of himself and the situation as he began to drive the truck up the highway. He didn't accelerate any more than he had before the attack. He kept a cool head and a calm hand on the wheel.

"It was a pretty amateur operation, don't you think?" Valters asked after a bit. "You'd have thought they'd do it better, have the roadblock somewhere more convenient for their reinforcements."

"Are there roads into the city that are closer to any of the militia barracks?" Nile asked coolly. He already knew the answer.

"Oh, yes. But I didn't take those roads. That would have been foolish of me. I knew that this was the least populated route into Riga from the farm."

"Then it isn't really that surprising that the militia would be so unprepared there, is it? Not if you had already studied their natural weaknesses and were playing off them."

Janis nodded and smiled a bit. "Some thought does pay off. It's like playing a concert and knowing who's going to be in your audience. If it's a certain kind of group, then you must work around their prejudices and their likes and their dislikes, beginning strong, if that's the best way to go, or soft, if that's their mood."

"You just did the same thing, but in your own way."

"Yeah, I suppose so."

"It's a good thing that Peteris gave us some of his clothes," Nile said, studying the peasant garb he had on. "We could be in trouble if I were sitting up here with you in a uniform."

"That would make things interesting. I'm afraid I have to admit that your size and that nearly white hair of yours makes you stand out even more than I'm comfortable with. But any notice you get should just be due to common interest. There's nothing to say that you are absolutely not Latvian. Claude, that would be another story. I have very few dark-skinned country-men!"

"Hayes and Billy Two we will rely on only in the dark, when their complexions aren't clearly visible. They understand that. There have been operations when the roles were reversed, when my own white skin would have given us away, so I had to hide myself."

"You make the racial issues sound so unimportant," Janis said, almost combatively. "Even the Swedish media, the neutrals, say it is the cancer in your country, the way that people who aren't of European descent have been treated."

"I won't deny that there are parts of our history that have been pretty dismal on that count," Nile said. He was being very cautious. Janis was showing a little more interest in the United States and, despite sounding contrary, he didn't have as negative an opinion of the U.S. as he'd had in the morning.

"But we struggle, all of us, to deal with what's going on now. Claude Hayes is a member of my team. The fact that he's a black man doesn't even register in my mind. Billy Two is a full-blooded Osage. He takes great pride in that, but he never forgets that he's also an American and that he's also a member of the SOBs. We work with what we have, and we do the best job we can. The important thing is that we know there's work to be done, and we do it."

"You talk about people as though they have many parts to themselves," Janis said softly.

"And they do. So long as they're happy with them and they don't interfere with the rest of their lives, then they should be able to celebrate all of them, just the way we celebrate all of our ethnic diversity in the U.S.

"You know, I bet that Alex Nanos makes just as big a deal out of his Greek heritage as Claude or Billy Two do of theirs. The rest of us actually feel a little cheated that we don't have that kind of firm grasp of where we came from. Except for being Americans, of course. But I think a lot of Americans wish they had a concrete footing to stand on from their past the way that Claude and Billy Two do. It's something we're all beginning to understand as very important and very positive."

"I doubt there are any people in your country who would find being Latvian a very important thing."

"Don't be so sure," Nile said. "I bet you money there are people who believe just that."

JANIS HAD BEEN RIGHT. It never did any good for Barrabas to try to hide his height. No man who stood more than six feet four inches could make himself seem short, and any time any person attempted to alter that kind of image he only drew more attention to himself than he would have otherwise. It was a simple lesson, and one that Barrabas had learned well.

He and Janis walked easily and comfortably through the crowds on the streets of Riga.

The lingering summer warmth had brought out people who gladly thronged on the streets or gathered in animated groups on the street corners. Evidently everyone regarded the balmy weather as an opportunity to store in the memory such days for the cold, relentless winter.

Once in a while passersby would look more closely at the tall white-haired man in homespun-style clothes and at his young companion, dressed in black from head to toe. Then the moment of curiosity passed, and they idly turned their eyes elsewhere.

After a succession of progressively larger buildings with the air of being public edifices, Janis slowed his steps somewhat. "There's the Naval Institute," Janis said as they approached an ornate building. It was clearly a temple to the bureaucracy, with a lot of decoration. Nile was especially interested in the vast lawn that surrounded the structure on all sides. That could be a big plus.

"They'd like us to think there was a lot of construction going on," Valters said, "but I've never seen those workmen before."

"Could they be imported from Moscow? Are they doing such specialized labor that the local folk wouldn't have the skills or the security clearances?"

"No." Janis was studying the gangs of laborers who were clustered on the lawn around the building. Something seemed to be puzzling him. "I know some of them, I'm sure of that, but it seems as though they're in the wrong place or something."

Barrabas knew just how to deal with that. "Then they probably are in the wrong place. Try changing their clothing, try putting them in different contexts. It's an old but true trick of the trade. Visualize them as anything but what they are."

"Militia." Valters was adamant. "As soon as I use my mind to change their clothing, I see them in uniforms. They must be on a special detail guarding the Panther you want so badly."

"It should be expected that the Russians would take special precautions. How many of them do you think there are?"

"Look! It's not just that they're the wrong people—that they're out of uniform—but the longer we stand here, the more clearly I can see that they aren't really doing any work. They're only pretending to be busy. None of them are real. How many? I would have thought about twenty-five at first, but now I think there are many more."

"We're going to have to go in there when it's dark. We'll need all the elements of surprise that night can give us."

"There'll be a moon, but that's all," Janis said as he continued to sweep the area with his eyes. "The midnight shift will have to have fewer men on it."

"Are they Latvians, then? Will that be a problem for you, fighting your countrymen?" He was wondering if the firefight at the checkpoint was eating away at the young man.

Janis turned to Nile with cool determination. "It had to be done for a greater and more immediate cause. Even if they didn't want to, those men had no choice but to obey the authorities. Some obey more willingly than others—that's human nature—and I'm sorrier for some than for others. Can't be helped.

"But the real traitors, Barrabas, they are my special target. I want them worse than I want the Russians.

"Elisabeth and the other old people talk about the collaborators who worked with the Nazis. In my own family I know there were Latvians who turned their own countrymen in to Stalin's henchmen. These turncoats, these men and women who care so little about their homeland that they would sell its children and its patriots to our invaders, are the darkest part of our life in Latvia. Like bad seeds, they appear in every generation. I have no problems with dealing with them, Barrabas. I only want them in the sights of my guns and their necks in my fists. I want to cleanse Latvia with their blood."

The young man made an about-face and began to march past the crowds of people, going toward Knighthood Square, their next stop.

Nile kept pace with Janis but let him have some time alone to cope with that rush of anger he'd just expressed. Barrabas understood what such emotions were like. They weren't feelings that a man wanted to share with anyone else at the moment of their eruption.

They were wonderful things to know about your allies, though, Barrabas thought, summing up the situation in his mind. Their appearance made Barrabas trust Valters all the more. The man would *fight*, and he was going to be on the SOBs team. It never hurt to know what strong motivations your partners felt.

13

"That park around the Naval Institute is going to work to our advantage," Barrabas said as he and Janis sat at Valters's favorite café in Knighthood Square. "There'll be at least some noise with the plan I have, and the space between the building and the nearest residences gives us a good buffer."

"Yes," Janis said, "but even noise wouldn't necessarily be a cause for concern. The institute deals with large machinery, and everyone here knows that. So long as there's no alarm sent in to the militia, there may be no problem." He fell quiet for a moment as a noisy group lingered by the table on their way out.

"But how do we make sure that there's no one free to send out that alarm?" Barrabas resumed the conversation.

"My people have been watching the building regularly. Those fake workers must be a new tactic; they hadn't been reported to me before. I can check with those I know who understand the workings of the inside of the Naval Institute. They were the real janitors and grounds keepers. They can confirm if my judgment about the people on the grounds was correct. Until they tell us otherwise, I have a good picture of the setup inside the building. The head of the operation is a newcomer, a man named Geogi.''

Nile looked away, abstractedly taking stock of the people around them as he digested that news.

''I know him,'' he said, and his only other response was a fleeting hard look in his eyes that sent a shiver down Janis's spine. ''I didn't know he was actually on the scene. The last I had heard he was in the United States.''

''No. He came over as soon as the shipment arrived. Obviously he's the one who's in charge. He works all hours—he might well still be in there after midnight. So, too, might the scientists. They're working double shifts and taking odd times off to rest. The navy keeps a detachment of twenty uniformed men in the building at all times. There are three teams of two who regularly patrol the park space around the building. We will have to eliminate them first, and do it so quickly and quietly that we arouse no suspicion inside. There are then fourteen naval guards in the building. I have memorized the floor plan, which I can draw for you when we get back to my loft and you will be able to see their locations. They apparently are very good about blindly following their orders and stay at their posts.''

Barrabas leaned forward across the table to give his words greater emphasis. ''That's good news,'' he said, ''but we shouldn't underestimate them. Still, I know it can be a help for surprise moves when soldiers have been discouraged from thinking for themselves.''

''I thought you'd think so. Now, these others, the new ones, I'm not sure what could be happening with them at night. They clearly can't be keeping up their act of working on the structure when there's no light. We'll have to assume that they're still inside, armed, and are waiting for us. From my plans, we can make very good guesses as to where they'll be. Some of these men, if they are local militia, have no more originality than a rodent. They will be looking for the place where they can be lazy and slothful—probably where they can be drinking."

"But that's too many people to spread apart." Nile thought quickly. "I wish we knew more about the intelligence of the security system in the building. The safest way to go would be to cut out the telephone lines completely, from the outside. We can't take that chance without knowing whether that would set off its own alarm, one even more dangerous to us."

Janis contemplated the problem for a moment. "I have someone on the inside of the telephone agency. I can reach him this evening and see if he can't arrange it." Janis smiled at Barrabas. "It is hardly news when a part of the telephone system breaks down. It's almost expected. If we had repairmen with proper credentials on the scene, it wouldn't cause any suspicion at all."

"This is the system of government that can put men on the moon and satellites in the heavens?" Barrabas laughed. "I shouldn't be surprised, the U.S. has its own problems with those kinds of little things. It's the big things like nuclear bombs the superpowers do so well."

He picked up his glass of tea and began to sip it while his eye casually swept across the plaza and suddenly spotted a woman. Beautiful. Exotic. Self-confident, with all the assurance of grace. He was stunned into silence. It was her!

He had never considered the possibility that she would be there. He knew that Geogi was, and that really hadn't been a surprise. It only made sense that the top guy in an operation of such magnitude would see the whole thing through to completion. And if he was there, why wouldn't he bring his woman along.

Barrabas swore he could smell her scent as he saw the dignified walk and the way her scarf flew in the air. She was older, her body lacked the hard lines it used to have, but that didn't hide her identity. Nothing could have.

Sophia would always look that good to him. She didn't seem to look over in his direction. If she had, she hadn't noticed him at all. Why would he expect her to recognize him now? It had been many years. Just because she'd crept back into his mind regularly didn't mean that she had to have any painful memories of her own.

She had been a professional, after all, trained to hide her true feelings and probably adept at cleansing herself of unproductive remembrances.

White-mouthed, Barrabas looked away.

"Are you all right?" Janis asked.

"Yeah, sure," Barrabas answered unconvincingly. "Look, we better get back to your place and fill in the rest of the team."

Barrabas stood up. He obviously didn't want to discuss that decision. Janis shrugged and silently agreed. He threw some money on the table to pay for their refreshments, and then the two men left the carefree crowds in Knighthood Square and began to wend their way through the narrow streets of the old city toward Janis's loft.

NILE PULLED ON HIS SHIRT and then walked over to the table to go through the plans of the Naval Institute once more. True to his word, Janis had been able to reconstruct the layout of the building with admirable detail. The institute was four stories tall, but the ground level and the top floor were both dedicated to uses they wouldn't have to be concerned with.

The open space on the first floor was mainly for public purposes, with higher ceilings than the others to accommodate and give the proper atmosphere for ceremonial functions. It was a natural gathering place for most of the guards. From there, they could control the entrances and exits of the building without bothering the scientists who were working on the second and third floors.

Those were the places where the Panther would have to be located. The top floor of the building housed mainly the utilitarian aspects of the operation—the secretaries' offices and storerooms.

The team was dressed, waiting for the word to move. Janis burst back through the door of his loft, all smiles.

"I've arranged for the telephones to go off-line at one o'clock this morning. The repairmen will show up almost at once, and we'll be in their van with them. It's unusual for services to be rendered so quickly, but I think everyone will simply be too relieved to question it too closely. I also went and talked to a man I know who works as a janitor in the building. Let me show you—"

Janis went over to the plans Nile had been studying and pointed to the second floor. "This is probably where your machine is. The Latvian civilian staff has been forbidden access to that area, and it's here—" he pointed to a small room off to the side of the larger laboratory "—that Geogi has his office. There will have to be a staff guard for Geogi, but I have no idea how large. The naval guard is all on the first floor, always. During the day they're like statues, never moving from their assigned posts. At night they must be more lax. My man tells me there are always leftover foods and wrappers strewn around the place. They must be snacking and eating during the night when there are fewer superiors around.

"The third floor is where the regular work of the institute is going on. Unless some people get that far as a refuge, there'll be no reason to worry about it."

"We still have the guards outside to worry about, besides the fourteen naval guards on the first floor and an undetermined number of other security forces on the second floor." Barrabas turned to Claude Hayes and Lee Hatton, who were studying the layout over his shoulder. "What do you think?"

"I think Billy Two and me can do some Indian tricks on those suckers outdoors. The telephone people, as Janis said, will be just as valuable as distractions as they will be in taking care of outside contact."

Claude turned to his friend. "Billy, you up for a game of slingshot? We got to have quiet on our side in the beginning. Even these slowed-down guns that the boss has us using aren't enough. But some good hard slingshots, that could really do a nice silent trick."

"With sharp weapons," Billy Two said thoughtfully, "we could work together, make sure we got a pair at a time."

Lee Hatton looked with awe at Barrabas as the plan began to unfold. She was just fully recognizing what an outrageous mission the colonel had led them on. He was a shrewd man with excellent judgment and extreme daring when needed—and handsome to boot. Surprised by her own train of thought, she smiled at her feminine response to him.

"Easy as pie. All we need are some good heavy elastic bands, some pieces of wood to carve with—"

"I have it all," Janis announced. "I'm just not sure about your just using such a primitive weapon."

"We're just primitive men," Claude laughed, "the most primitive in the world. Billy Two and me have used these things before. Technology is fine, but sometimes simple things work best. Rest on it, Janis, we can fire a slingshot like David did to slay Goliath, and we're a lot bigger than that sucker was, and they're a lot smaller than Goliath. We got some hours before we move. It's enough time to make the tools."

"Go with it," Barrabas said. "But technology is going to be our weapon for the rest of it, especially taking out the naval guard on the first floor and preparing for any of the Latvian militia. We need something to negate fourteen men as quickly as possible, quickly enough for us to get to the next floor and deal with whoever's there before they know what's happened to them."

Barrabas turned to Beck. "Then you have to go to it. I'll do everything I can to get you the time, Nate, but it's going to be damned hard. Go for the real inside stuff, and make sure you're ready to blow the entire machine if it's necessary. I want the mission accomplished. I don't want any unnecessary deaths. We'll hold the fort while you get the thing done."

"Fast as I can, Nile."

"It's all that I can ask. The best job you can do."

THE PAINT WAS BACK on their faces. The grease, the cold, clammy grease, made them remember what they were, who they were, what they were doing.

Riga was a soft place that night. There was no wind off the gulf, and the August warmth still enveloped the city. There was an eerie feeling in the air, a deeper-than-usual silence.

The hour had much to do with that. There was no traffic at that hour. Nightclubs in the Soviet empire close early, and the illegal revelers who mocked the anti-alcohol drive from Moscow with their endless stills pouring out rivers of moonshine were hidden away outside the center of town, drawing the riffraff of Riga with them.

Barrabas and the rest of the team were in the back of a van that carried the emblem of the local telephone agency. There was a danger in trusting all these locals with their lives. They could be double agents, any or all of them could have just been biding their time before they turned on Janis, and the coup of finding the American marauders would be just the perfect justification for that kind of thing.

Barrabas thought back to that small group in front of the United Nations and to the profile in courage they'd shown him, and he trusted. He trusted that the passion for liberty that Janis and Elisabeth spoke of was enough to make people like these take enormous gambles.

There was a pounding on the back door of the van. In a moment, Janis opened the doors and waved Claude and Billy Two out into the night to start taking out the guards on the grounds.

The rest of them gave their friends a soundless salute. They began a wordless countdown that wouldn't end until the battle was over, and it amounted to a prayer to whatever image of God they believed in.

HAWK SPIRIT FLEW in the night, having come to life in the body of ravens that circled the Naval Institute. Billy Two looked up at the sky and saw them clearly through his Starlite goggles.

The glasses seemed magic and felt right to him. A night bird can see in the dark, and he was in flight with the black scavengers that screeched their signals from above. Hawk Spirit was with them, in them, part of them. Just as the scope gave Billy Two sight beyond the ability of most humans, Hawk Spirit guided his soul, lifted him up, prepared to take his missiles and guide them in the night.

Billy Two smiled at the idea of the pieces of wood and metal sporting a sharp point that he and Claude had shaped earlier as missiles to be used to save an ultramodern piece of technology. These were the tools of his ancestors, the ones Hawk Spirit had given to the Osage to help them in battle, before there had been white men, before there had been borders to fight over, before there had been anything but man, his prey and the earth.

Claude Hayes moved, silent and liquid in the way he flowed with the night. Billy Two and his unseen, all-seeing Hawk Spirit approved of the way the huge black man could glide along the surface of the earth on just the balls of his feet, never making hard noises on pavement, never interfering with even the leaves of a tree as he moved past it.

Claude motioned to Billy Two with his hand. There was a target. Two men in formal uniforms marched with great precision along the far southern corner of the plot of ground.

As though they were two dancers who'd practiced their steps together for years, Claude and Billy Two lifted up the large slings and sighted. These weren't the small things that boys played with. These were the weapons of men, deadly when they were handled with great accuracy.

With the help of Hawk Spirit, there could be nothing but accuracy.

The slings were retracted backward as far as they could be. The muscles in their arms twitched from the labor of holding the heavy industrial rubber in place. The lethal missile in the pouch played in Billy Two's hands. Claude nodded once, and simultaneously they let their packages fly into the night.

Billy Two watched as the guards staggered from the sudden, totally unexpected blows. They'd landed perfectly. The sharp wood had pierced their skulls. There was only the slightest moan from one of them, and they dropped to the ground.

Billy Two raced to the bodies, his knife in his hand now. He leaned over and with quick slashes of the knife finished them off.

He wasn't being cruel. Only a fool would have condemned him for the act of mercy. The missiles probably had done the job, but if they'd been off only by a fraction, the men could have lingered on to succumb finally to a death slow and painful beyond imagination.

The stroke of the blade was the Osage's last gesture to a fallen foe.

Billy Two took the lead now, not waiting for Claude to make the motions that directed them to the next team. It was night, and the night belonged to Hawk Spirit, who crowed through the mouths of the black ravens still flying above.

They raced almost silently across the lawn, rushing to be in position to take out the next pair of sentries. They saw them, raised their slings and sent the missiles flying. The targets were found. Billy Two's blade dripped blood. The ravens screamed more loudly.

Being filled with a terrible grimness, the two men moved on to their next target.

"DONE." THAT WAS ALL Claude Hayes said when they climbed back into the van.

"The telephone lines have been cut. Our guys are inside causing a ruckus," Alex said.

It was Nile Barrabas who picked up on the expression in Claude's eyes when the goggles were removed. He put a hand on Hayes's shoulder and squeezed tightly. No words needed to be said: the colonel knew of the terrible and taxing task.

Billy Two's extremely remote expression began to fade, and he opened his mouth and tilted back his head as though he were letting out a cry of the wild.

But he kept his silence, the silence the team had to have to survive the moment.

Nile saw the gesture and could have sworn that Billy Two's open mouth looked like the beak of a predatory bird. There were times when the Osage seemed to actually take on the visage of his spirit.

Barrabas felt a chill, even in the summer air and in the confines of the van, and he felt whatever Claude Hayes was experiencing. But he wouldn't talk about it. A leader had to deal with his troops, not with their gods.

"Time for the next act. As soon as the telephone repairmen come out, we go in."

The next tap on the door was from Janis, and it was the sign they were waiting for. They were ready, and made brief eye contact. Touching base before pitching themselves headlong into the fight, a fight that some of them might not survive.

Only a fool goes into battle without emotions. Sometimes those emotions were the tightrope on which Billy Two balanced as he sorted out his two personalities. Other times it was the vengeance sweeping through Nile Barrabas as he thought of Geogi. Years of anger could be wiped out in the next few hours, a measure of repayment could be exacted.

Alex Nanos chewed gum and wondered if this was the time he'd get it. That thought wandered through his mind as it did every time he was ready to fight, because there had to be one time too many, one time when he was going to bite it. He looked over at Liam O'Toole and wondered about the Irishman. Would he just be composing poetry now? Was that what happened to Liam when he was facing the big battle?

Lee Hatton wondered how she managed to create her own balance, her own peace with the contradictions of her life. She hefted the H&K machine pistol in her arms and considered yet again her pledge as a physician to heal. Could the gun coexist with her vow to save lives?

Nate Beck didn't have those problems. He wasn't worrying about his soul in some way, or his emotions, or his peace. He was thinking about the machines. It was essential he train his mind and get it into the proper concentration to deal with the task in a detached and objective manner. He went over and over the diagrams of the Panther that he'd been studying since they'd left New York. There were so many parts of it that were unique and delicate, but they had to be taken out. It was a must. He ran his brain as he would one of his computers back in Connecticut. Perhaps that was his own way of handling what was about to happen.

"Go."

Barrabas only said the one word, and the team piled out of the van and moved up toward the door of the institute. They all had knapsacks on their shoulders. The plans they had memorized came to life as they got closer to the structure. They could see all the details that Janis had carefully schooled them on. Nile and Nate Beck headed for the front entrance. Billy Two and Claude held back, their H&Ks ready. Lee and Liam O'Toole went to the rear door, and Nanos followed Janis to the one side entrance.

Their watches had been synchronized. Nile and Nate reached into their packs, and each one drew out a pyrotech M-880, a flash-bang grenade. They studied their watches and commenced a countdown. Then they activated the grenades and tossed them, shattering the glass as the payloads sped into the building.

The flash-bangs burst into a startlingly visual explosion. The phosphorus-loaded grenades made no more noise than small firecrackers, but they gave off what seemed to be as much light as the sun itself.

The naval guards were stunned by the flash. They were blinded, every one of them. The shock of the unexpected incendiary bombs left them unable to move, and the few who tried were disoriented in the extreme and stumbled and fell.

The doors were open now, but the guards couldn't move to defend them. Almost all the AK-47s were scattered around the room. Only two men held their automatic rifles in their hands, and they began to discharge them wildly into the night. Still unable to see, they shot wherever they could, knowing only the fear of trapped animals.

The SOBs' H&Ks began a softer chatter in answer, cutting down the guards one by one. The two with rifles were so panicked and their fire so erratic that they were no threat to the team, but they did manage to cut down some of their own comrades.

Billy Two was able to walk right up to the back of one of the riflemen and deliver a short burst of fire right into his head, another coup de grace, another offering to an honorable foe.

Claude Hayes grabbed the AK-47 out of the other man's hands and left the Russian sailor flailing at the air, still blind. Claude used the butt of the gun to knock the man out, sending him sprawling unconscious on the floor.

Only seconds had passed, but the sounds of the AK-47 had to have alerted anyone left in the building. Alex Nanos was the first one to reach the stairs and charge up them.

At the top of the stairs, a dumbfounded guard stood, unable to believe that anyone was actually assaulting the building. It took him a second to organize all the stimuli, make sense of all the things that were happening in front of him. It was a second too long, and it was all Nanos needed to fire the H&K and topple the man from the head of the stairs.

O'Toole was right behind Alex, and they got to the landing at the same time. Their machine pistols spit out deadly rounds of hot lead at three men on the run to see what the commotion was. The trio went down quickly without being able to get off a shot.

The rest of the team pounded up the stairs right behind Alex and Liam. Pausing expectantly with quivering nerves and reflexes that would be set off instantaneously, they scanned the area opening before them, their ready guns attuned to their senses.

14

The familiar sound of the automatic rifle penetrated Geogi's office. He jumped up and went to his desk to grab his own AK-47, then grabbed the telephone, only to slam it down quickly. Things were looking bad, he acknowledged to himself.

"What is it?" Sophia asked, startled by the series of explosions and by Nikoli's quick reaction.

"Trouble" was all he'd say.

Sophia stood up from her chair and moved toward the door.

"Get away from there!" Nikoli commanded.

Pressing her back to the wall, she slid to one side. Her eyes were wide, but not in fear, just in wonder. She was no novice. She had seen plenty of action before Geogi had taken away her prized status and relegated her to the role of kept woman.

They listened as the AK-47 fire alternated with something much less noisy. "Silencers?" she whispered to him.

"No." He was clearly puzzled, but then realized the answer. "Subcaliber rounds. The bullets aren't crossing the sound barrier. They'd lose some of their effect at long range, but close up, in good hands, they'd still be deadly."

"Who could it be?" She didn't understand how a carefully guarded research center in the center of a Soviet city could be a target for any action.

"The Americans, they must be trying one of their desperate actions."

"No! Not in Latvia!"

"Then who else do you think?" Geogi sneered at the woman. "Dissidents from the Politburo?"

Just then the gunfire stopped altogether. Nikoli went to the door that connected the office to the hallway outside and, with his back pressed against the wall on the opposite side of the portal from Sophia, leaned forward to listen closely.

He motioned for her to keep quiet. Damn the woman! He'd had her come over only for some recreational sex, a little break in the monotony of his work, and now he was anchored with her in the middle of whatever was going on.

Finally some very faint whispers reached his ears. Geogi couldn't make the words out, but by then he was convinced he would have to contend with the Americans.

He pulled up the AK-47 and got ready. Someone was coming through—there was no question. Geogi's finger tightened on the trigger. There was a slight movement on the doorknob, and then the door flew open. Geogi waited just a moment, wanting to make sure of his target and what might be behind him. A flicker of movement caught his eye. Then an object rolled into the room. A grenade? Panic swept through Nikoli; then he saw the small metal container burst into unbelievable light. He was blinded! There was nothing but searing brightness in his eyes.

He felt the panic of a wounded animal. His finger twitched, and the AK-47 began to belch bullets into the air. He moved, trying to remember just where the doorway was, and tried to fire through it, sending out waves of lead. Then he felt a procession of indescribable points of pain that seemed to run from his waist up to his stomach, through his chest.

Nikoli Geogi died before he understood that the pains were American bullets cutting a line up toward his heart.

"BLAST! DID I—"

"No," Lee Hatton said as she knelt over the dead woman, "these are from his AK-47. He must have panicked when the incendiary bomb went off and he shot, only guessing where he was aiming. She was in his field of fire, that's all."

Liam O'Toole stood back from the doorway and wiped the sweat off his forehead. Death was never beautiful when he caused it, and it seemed to him that the woman had been an innocent victim of a war in which he only followed his orders and had nothing to do with the decisions that led to battle. The images of women and children caught between maneuvering armies swamped Liam's memory, and each of them brought a slight nausea.

Lee took the woman's thick sable coat and threw it over her body, covering her face.

"Pull it back," Nile Barrabas demanded from the doorway.

Lee looked up at him, startled by his harsh tone. She didn't think she'd ever heard Nile talk to her that way.

There was something steely in his eyes as he stared at the cadaver. Lee felt a shiver move through her body.

She reached up and pulled the sable down from the woman's beautiful face. She turned back to Nile and waited for a reaction.

Barrabas staggered against the door frame. The color drained from his face as his hand came up to cover his eyes. For the first time in her life, Lee Hatton thought Nile might shed real tears.

He turned away after only a couple of beats of time. With his back to the door, he began to bellow orders to the other men on the floor, directing Billy Two and Nanos up the stairs to make sure there weren't any more hidden enemies, telling Nate Beck to get a move on, there was no time for anything but work.

Liam and Lee looked at one another and forgot whatever response they themselves had to the carnage in the Naval Institute. They had just witnessed something incredible in those seconds of response from Nile Barrabas, something that they knew was remarkable.

DAWN WAS STILL HOURS AWAY. They had been on top alert for the time right after their assault, worried that the noise of the gunfire might have aroused the suspicions of any passersby. But no one had come. The police hadn't been in the vicinity. There were no residential buildings nearby. The lights in the Naval Institute caused no concern, and anyone who saw only them and hadn't heard the firefight, which had lasted only a few minutes, wasn't curious. The scientists in the place regularly worked all hours.

The rest of them were still jumpy, but Billy Two was actually serene as he paced the perimeter of the institute grounds. He and Liam O'Toole had fit into the uniforms of the two largest naval guards. As part of the cover, they'd put them on and had been marching together in an endless walk around the parklike expanse of lawn that surrounded the building.

Liam succumbed to small involuntary tremors. The adrenaline was still coursing through him, but he'd had to slow down for the time being. The anxiety that all of them felt in the midst of this dangerous, lingering mission must be getting to the other man, Billy Two thought.

Staying inside a Soviet government building in the middle of a provincial capital was hardly the safest thing they could do. Being on the move in enemy territory was bad enough, but at least the mobility gave them something extra, a sense of being in motion, while this kind of operation only left them with the sense of being powerless targets if they were ever found out.

None of that was of concern to Billy Two. He did his imitation with great seriousness, knowing that the intensity would help him swiftly swing into action again when needed.

There was almost no traffic on the streets, and the occasional delivery van or police car didn't even slow down to check them out. Billy Two knew they wouldn't.

Hawk Spirit was with him. He looked up in the sky and saw that the ravens were always there, protecting him. He was convinced they were hanging a curtain of invisibility over the operation. There was no danger, because the spirits wanted them all to be safe and secure. They would succeed because the gods were with them. Billy Two was sure of it.

But that didn't mean he ever took his finger off the trigger of the AK-47 he'd taken from a Russian corpse, nor did he forget that his uniform had a bullet hole cut cleanly through the fabric, right above his heart, where the Russian who'd owned it had taken his mortal wound.

Billy Two might fly with the ravens and talk to Hawk Spirit, but he never denied the realities of earth.

JANIS WAS OCCUPYING the reception desk of the Naval Institute. He had no god to whom he could appeal for protection. Nothing was with him but his mortal fear that all of this would blow up. The American mercenaries were heroic and capable, there was no doubt about it, and the network of people who were loyal to the idea of a free Latvia had all done their jobs with precision and with bravery.

The telephone men he'd used were on their way back to Rezekne, near the Russian border. He'd known better than to use people in Riga: they'd have been too easily found out. On his orders, and not really knowing why, the men and women who were in the telephone service in the city and who were also working with him had made themselves conspicuous during the night in the clubs and restaurants. They would all have dozens of witnesses that they had not been part of the scheme.

The people from Rezekne wouldn't be so suspect; their stories didn't have to be so elaborate. They had come in to Riga in their uniforms and they'd arrived at the institute right on schedule. Then they'd quickly gone back home.

Still, there were many people involved, and they still had to wait.

"It's the worst part of it, kid," Alex Nanos said as he stood by Janis in another one of the Soviet naval uniforms. Nanos was there to give some firepower to back up the guy's stories, just in case there were too many sticky questions.

"The waiting," Nanos explained, as though he could read Janis's mind. But it wasn't that, not really. "It's the thing that gets to every military man, just waiting. The worst is in a big battle, the kind where you know damn well the enemy's going to attack as soon as the sun comes up. That's the worst, the worst ever."

The phone had been reconnected, without the security lines that fed directly into the militia headquarters. It rang and Janis answered it, hoping he would give the right responses.

"What was it?" Alex asked when Janis had hung up.

Janis smiled, but it was a tight smile. "A woman wanted to know when her man would be off duty; she wanted to cook him breakfast."

Nanos started to pace, and Janis looked through the directory on the desk to familiarize himself with the names. There was a spell of time ahead of them, and how long that would turn out to be depended on Nate Beck.

THE AMERICAN COMPUTER EXPERT worked feverishly on the Panther. He'd already taken out four of the six elements that had to be transported back to the United States.

He was gleeful about his work. He didn't think once about the danger involved in sitting in a laboratory in the middle of the Soviet empire. He was consumed with admiration for the technicians who'd built this thing.

"I tell you, Nile, Continental must have some of the top minds from MIT and Cal Tech to put this together. It's a work of art." Solving the beautifully intricate puzzle was making his day. "Those Russkies, they had only begun to figure this out."

"You had the plans, Nate," Barrabas said. The constant talk coming from the small man was getting on his nerves. There wasn't much room in Barrabas's head for tolerance right then. There was too much going on inside him for him to give very much to other people.

That didn't mean Nile was falling apart. It was only during those fleeting moments in the doorway when he'd seen Sophia's dead body that he'd lost any of his consummate self-control. He was still the commander in the field, and he still had to be ready for anything that might come up.

But he was human, and right then he felt that fact more than he had in a long, long time.

What got to him most was the knowledge that he'd never had a last conversation with Sophia. He had never been able to ask her just what had gone on in her mind.

Would that have changed things? he wondered.

Maybe she would have told him that she really had been playacting her way through their affair. Could he have lived with that? Was the other possibility better, the thought that what had gone on between them had been real? And how would it all have mattered to him?

The simple fact was that he'd never know. He would continue wondering about what might have been and about what had never been. That was the source of the pain that caused the pounding in his brain. He would never know.

AT FOUR O'CLOCK, Barrabas went down to the front of the building. He went outdoors and motioned Billy Two and Liam O'Toole back inside. When they had stepped into the interior, he spoke to the whole group, which had congregated around the reception desk. "He's finished finally. Nate's packing the components for us to carry them. We have to go to the next step in the operation."

"I'm ready," Janis said, then picked up the phone and dialed a number. He spoke quickly in Latvian and hung up. "And so is our escape route, the prime one. There'll be another van here soon, in less than a half hour. Then we're going to the waterfront. From there, a boat will take you out of Russian waters."

"And you're coming with us," Nile announced. He knew that sometime during the night the young man must have made the only decision possible for him. Sooner or later, the KGB would catch up with him. But he was still reluctant and felt the need to protest.

"Barrabas, my country, people like Elisabeth..."

"The rest of your helpers may get away. It's your pals in the militia who're going to take the real heat for what has happened. But your days spent on our side have too many numbers on them. The odds are moving way against you, kid, and it's time for you to own up to that. The U.S. owes you. You owe yourself."

"I can't be sure.... The people who've helped with this operation are mine, my people!"

"Your music, Janis." Liam O'Toole walked up to the desk and put one of his big fists down on top of it. "I know about that, how important that is. Do you really dare believe that *glasnost* will last long enough for you to do your music? The ups and downs of the politics in Moscow aren't the most secure thing in the world, and you know it. You have an obligation to your art."

The Irishman did know what that was about, and all the humiliations and manipulations he'd been exposed to in his life as an aspiring poet didn't change a thing. The artist in a man can't be denied: it has a special kind of spirituality, and it has to be fed.

Janis stared at the Irishman's intense face, and dozens of thoughts flashed through his mind. There were the people whom he'd leave behind and the idea of being separated from the emerging new wave of interest in Latvian history and culture. But he'd not be much use dead.

Nate Beck came running down the stairs. "Ready! The pieces are packed and we're set to go." At that moment, Billy Two walked out through the front door of the institute and returned with a man in fisherman's garb from the waterfront.

"Know him?" Billy Two asked.

Janis looked at his friend Mikelis and nodded. "He's fine. He's your ticket out." He looked over at Nile Barrabas and then said, "He's *our* ticket out."

The van bore the name of a small fishing collective. Janis sat with the SOBs in the rear. They were carrying heavy loads, most with the parts from the Panther, the rest with double knapsacks loaded with all the other matériel and goods they had to get out of Latvia.

The van stopped and then made a series of backward and forward motions, obviously parking. Janis was nearest the driver's seat. The rear was separated from the front only by a makeshift panel, which was a blanket hung from hooks on the sides, just enough to give the human cargo cover but not enough to arouse suspicion.

The driver spoke in Latvian, and Janis nodded when he got the message. "We're here. The boat is only a few feet away. He's going to get out and make sure nothing's come up. Wait, but only for a few minutes."

The SOBs had not only their own H&K machine pistols but had taken along AK-47s from the dead Russian guards. They all were ready for anything. But they were all hopeful that things would go smoothly.

The back doors opened, and the Latvian fisherman motioned for them to hurry. They only had to clamber over a short gangplank to get onto the boat. It was an old wooden fishing vessel, made for two or three people to handle. The hold was empty, and one by one the SOBs scurried down a rope ladder to land in the dark space.

"Uh, what a stink!" Nanos whispered.

Lee Hatton and Nate Beck got out handkerchiefs and put them over their noses. They huddled in the hold of the small boat, knowing that silence would still be advisable.

The top of the hold was covered with a hastily thrown tarpaulin, and they were in darkness until Nile got a battery-operated lamp out of his pack and turned it on to shed some diffuse light over the space.

Then the boat started its tippy motions, and they knew they were on their way.

When they felt the harbor had been left behind, O'Toole spoke up. "How long is it going to take?"

"Three hours, at least. Hopefully we'll get to the middle of the Baltic," Nile answered. "Remember, it's going to take at least an hour before we clear the Gulf of Riga. Whatever this guy's boat's got going for it, speed isn't the jewel in the crown."

The tiny engine's constant chorus of *put-put-put* brought home the leader's point.

"You know what our clothes are going to smell like after this? Do you know what *we're* going to smell like?" Nanos asked with a groan.

"Like a big anchovy pizza!" Claude Hayes said, and playfully punched at Nanos's shoulder.

Billy Two joined in. "With hair on it! And in constant danger of getting a big beer belly to chase it with!"

"Stop it! You guys! Get serious! What if we smell so bad none of the Swedish women will want to come near us? Huh? Have you thought of that? We're going to be in Sweden tonight, and we may have such a case of the bad stinks that—"

"No. We won't be in Sweden tonight," Nile said.

"What!" Nanos was horrified. Visions of buxom Swedish women had been flitting through his mind during the entire operation. He'd felt cheated when they hadn't gotten a shot at any of them on the way to Latvia, but he'd been sure that they'd have their chance on the way out.

"The Panther has to be back in the United States as soon as possible. A plane will be waiting for us at Stockholm airport. We load up the components, then we go with it, right back to New York."

"New York!" Janis said as visions of the great American metropolis lighted up his imagination.

"New York!" Nanos cried out, remembering the women there who were going to jump him for unanswered phone calls and broken dates. Manhattan was a very scary place for a man like him.

BILLY TWO AND O'TOOLE had been holed up in midtown Manhattan at a plush hotel. After the gourmet fare available in the luxurious establishment they had felt the desire for simpler and more solid food. So they had ordered in pizza and had themselves a good at-home kind of time.

They also had a program for fun at an East Village address, which wasn't the most friendly part of town, but still an "in" place. They were going to see Janis Valters's first performance in America.

"Let's go, Liam, the kid'll be waiting."

The two of them had dressed casually. Billy Two wore leather pants and a fringed leather vest without a shirt. Liam put on his camou pants. That was his own way of honoring Janis. He knew that the crowds in a place like the East Village wouldn't know the real ones—which they might have objected to politically—from the fake ones they loved to wear themselves. Just to add to the image, he pulled out a black leather jacket and put it on over his olive-drab Army-issue T-shirt.

Then they were ready and descended to the lobby level of the hotel in the elevator and ignored the stares they got as they walked out the main entrance to the waiting line of cabs. When they'd climbed into the first one in line, Billy Two pulled out a worn piece of paper from his pants pocket. "Let's see, we're going to Avenue B and—"

"Are you sure?" The cab driver certainly wasn't excited by the idea of his fare. Neither the look of the two guys nor their destination filled him with great confidence.

"We are very, very sure," Liam intoned, and his voice didn't leave any room for disagreement.

The driver took the paper from Billy Two and read it, shrugged and pulled out into the traffic, hoping that if there was going to be any trouble it would come while these two bozos were still with him. Let them take the heat. If nothing else, they looked like they'd know how to handle it.

The taxi went south through all the many and varied neighborhoods of Manhattan. The passengers talked excitedly about what was ahead, more about who they were going to see.

"Didn't he feel a whole lot better about leaving Latvia when he saw who took the fall for the operation?" Liam said.

"He was a damned smart operator, had to be, to survive that long, and it's a good thing he never let the skirt in on his plans. That could have really gotten him—and us—into lots of trouble."

"And all along he thought he was saving her from trouble by leaving her in the dark. If she didn't know anything, then there wasn't any way the KGB could get their mitts on her."

"Never knew that old Commie friend of his was putting it to her. Hell! But they're sitting in Siberia now, from what the papers say, blamed for the whole thing. Damn Russians don't even know it was us. That frosts me. I mean, we do all this stuff and never get any credit. Sometimes I think we should."

"Sure, but it wouldn't last long. Think of the hit teams that would be after us to get back for whatever we did," O'Toole said with a shudder.

"Yeah, yeah, but can't I dream? We are undercover all the time, but a little publicity would do us wonders. Think of the women Nanos could lay! And think of how much more money Jessup could charge if we were a name brand."

"'A name brand'?" Liam had to think about that one. "Lad, I'm afraid we'll have to stay faceless, like all the unwashed soldiers of history. We will persevere on just our valor."

"Bull—"

"Here you are, gents."

They didn't even look until they got out of the cab. Then they stared at the building. It couldn't be where they were going! But they knew it was. The inscription over the doorway said Latvian Culture Center.

BILLY TWO RAN HIS HANDS down over his hair in the kind of gesture people use when they feel slightly out of place. They'd been so convinced that their night would be one spent on the wild side of the East Village that neither of them had thought of any other possibility. They'd forgotten that the same neighborhood that contained the most avant-garde elements of the New York art and music scene had traditionally been one of the centers where immigrants from Europe congregated.

Although the neighborhood had more rock clubs per block than anywhere else in America, there was also an abundance of Ukrainian and Baltic restaurants.

Sheepishly the two men walked up the stairs, feeling very conspicuous in their outfits. They were greeted at the door by a smiling matron who graciously requested a two-dollar donation that, she told them, would be going to the artist. Billy Two upped his to twenty dollars, and Liam followed suit.

They took seats on folding chairs at the back of the auditorium and tried not to notice all the people staring at them. In time, Janis came on stage and gracefully bowed to the group. He sat down with his guitar and spoke to them in Latvian, which neither of the Americans could understand. The SOBs looked around to observe other members of the audience, and they could tell from the serious looks they saw that Janis was giving a serious concert.

He strummed his guitar, and echoes of the free Latvia moved through the room. The audience was obviously moved, and the strong sentiment aroused in individuals became an almost palpable thing.

Billy Two only heard the sounds, and he found in them something elemental that rose above all the separating influence of different languages and spoke to the emotions and longings that were basic needs shared by all people.

Liam listened only to the art and knew that there was poetry coming from Janis's fingers, sheer, beautiful, glorious poetry.

They didn't know that Nile Barrabas was also in the hall, standing in the back, in the doorway. He heard his own message, that there was a cry for freedom in the world, and as he looked around at the fighters who guarded it and the people who nurtured it, he knew that they could all be together in one place and listen to that cry only in a free country.

He was glad that Janis Valters was there to remind them, all Americans, of such elemental truths.

DON PENDLETON's

MACK BOLAN

**Everything has its price—
even all-out war.**

Bolan is pitted against a group of mercenaries who, fueled by Libyan funds, are planning an assault on the capital of Libya.

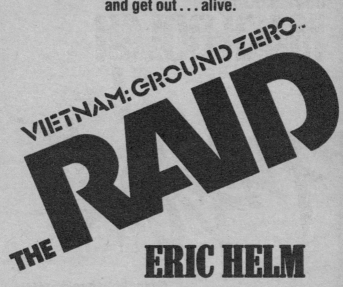